The Sacred Fire

BY THE SAME AUTHOR

Vengeance of the Oval Portrait

The Sacred Fire

by
Gabriel de Lautrec

Translated, annotated and introduced by
Brian Stableford

A Black Coat Press Book

ISBN 978-1-61227-876-6. First Printing: July 2019. Published by Black Coat Press, an imprint of Hollywood Comics.com, LLC, P.O. Box 17270, Encino, CA 91416. All rights reserved. Except for review purposes, no part of this book may be reproduced or transmitted in any form or by any means, electronic or mechanical, including photocopying, recording, or by any information storage and retrieval system, without permission in writing from the publisher. The stories and characters depicted in this novel are entirely fictional. Printed in the United States of America.

TABLE OF CONTENTS

Introduction

This is the second volume of samples from the work of Gabriel de Lautrec (1867-1938) to be published by Black Coat Press. The first, *The Vengeance of the Oval Portrait* (2011)[1] included the entire contents of his third collection of short prose items, *La Vengeance du portrait ovale* (1922), seven items from *Poèmes en prose* (1898) and six from *Histoires de Tom Joë* (1920). The present volume contains his short novel "Le Feu sacré" (tr. as "The Sacred Fire"), first published in the occult periodical *L'Initiation* in five episodes between December 1903 and June 1904, and all the items from *Poèmes en prose* not included in the earlier volume. The latter benefit from being juxtaposed with the short novel because one of the episodes of the novel reveals the circumstances in which they were composed, with not only explains their surreal nature but allows them to serve as an illustration of the argument made in that episode.

Maurice Magre recorded in one of his autobiographical essays that it was Gabriel Lautrec who first introduced him to the Occult Underworld of fin-de-siècle Paris shortly before 1900, by taking him to a séance in which "*ondins*" (water elementals)[2] were to be

---

[1] ISBN 978-1-61227-009-8.

[2] *Ondins* is a French equivalent of the word translated from the German into English as "undines," but in English they are invariably female, whereas on French they are often male, and when they are female are called *ondines*. The entities in question, as originally envisaged, were asexual, but in adapting

7

evoked. Magre reported that no *ondins* appeared and that he was unimpressed, but his autobiographical writings are not always trustworthy, and he later became one of the most assiduous *habitués* of that underworld, whereas Lautrec, although intensely interested and involved in it at one time, eventually abandoned it. For a period of some years, however, Lautrec was a dedicated lifestyle fantasist, at least part-time—he worked by day as a schoolteacher—and affected a flamboyant dandyism as well as decorating his apartment in a gaudily funereal fashion.

Lautrec eventually became best-known as a humorist, very much in the tradition established by his friend Alphonse Allais, but he first met Allais at *Le Chat Noir*, the favorite haunt of the Hydropaths, the Zutistes and other pillars of the Decadent Movement, and he was acquainted with the other regulars, including Jean Lorrain, another flamboyant dandy who had similar tastes in décor. He befriended Paul Verlaine before the latter's death, and Oscar Wilde also visited him at his home before his death. Although the three characters whose conversations and musings supply the content of *Le Feu sacré* are all versions of the author, they probably borrow elements from his literary acquaintances, and it is not improbable that "Saint-Maur" is partly modeled on Maurice Magre, just as Mathias Corbus borrows aspects of "Papus" (Gérard Encausse), the editor of *L'Initiation* and one of the leading figures of the French Occult Revival.

them to French literature they were typically divided as *sylphs / sylphides, gnomes / gnomides* and *salamanders / salamandrines*, in order to adapt them more easily to erotic fantasies.

Although "Le Feu sacré" opens with a description of the kind of "secret" ritual practiced by one of the numerous cults of the French Occult Revival, and much of the discussion featured in the story deals with the nature and philosophy of magic, the sequence that must have seemed most sensational at the time of its publication is its elaborate description of the effects of taking hashish in pill form, and its use as a source of literary inspiration.

Although such accounts had an august literary history in France, going back to Théophile Gautier's fictionalized description of "Le Club des haschichins" (1846), the experiments of which had provided the psychologist Joseph Moreau with information that he had adapted to a different purpose in his study *Du Hachisch et de l'aliénation mentale* (1845), and also gave Charles Baudelaire valuable raw material for the long essay "Le Poème du haschish" (1860 in *Les paradis artificiels*), little new empirical evidence from the viewpoint of a writer in search of inspirational aid had been added in more than half a century. Hallucinations credited to the use of hashish had featured in numerous entirely fanciful stories, and a number of stories based on psychotropically-induced fantasies had appeared, but even those plausibly represented as quasi-clinical descriptions, such as X. B. Saintine's "Les Hallucinations du docteur" (in *La Seconde Vie*, 1864;[3] tr. as "The Doctor's Hallucinations") are a trifle flimsy. Although Lautrec credits his monologue to a fictional characters, the book of *Poèmes en prose* he credits to that fictional character—"almost all" of which he claims were written under the influence of hashish—is obviously his own,

---

[3] Black Coat Press, ISBN 978-1-61227-750-9.

and the "fragment" to which Corbus refers specifically must be one of the items translated in the present volume.

Like Théophile Gautier's description of the effects of hashish, the one credited to Mathias Corbus is unlikely to seem recognizable to many contemporary users of cannabis, but Lautrec is careful to add the observation that the effects vary greatly, and depend to some extent on the existing mental state and the expectations of the user. In particular, he asserts that the effects of hashish intoxication will tend to reproduce the effects of other psychotropics that the user has employed, and offers that remark as an original observation.

Although Corbus claims to be familiar with both opium and ether, it is possible that Lautrec obtained much of his information about the former from Maurice Magre and the latter from Jean Lorrain, and it is possible that he encouraged both of them to try hashish, and observed the results. At any rate, Lautrec's account of the experiences that Corbus relates are an unusually elaborate account of the particular effects of the drug on one regular user, and the items added as supplements here provide a uniquely graphic example of the employment of cannabis-aided visions as literary source material by a writer of considerable talent.

The prose poems in question are among the most important precursors of surrealism, contemporary with the most important contributions that Alfred Jarry made to the preliminary foundations of that movement. Lautrec's interest in the hallucinations echoed in the prose poems also extended to a more general interest in dreaming, elaborately developed, in a suitably hallucinatory fashion, in the fourth chapter of "Le Feu sacré," in its remarkable account of the manner in which the author's acrophobia is inverted in a "compensatory" dream of a world underground before figuring speculatively as the seed of a hypothetical future religion. As with the previous episode, that chapter is a truly remarkable item of prose, all the more so as Lautrec seems to have concentrated thereafter, for the remainder of his active career, on humorous work, stories and verse for children, and translations.

"Le Feu sacré" was, in effect, the last gasp of a particular phase in his career, already marking a step into relative obscurity, having never achieved publication in volume form—or, indeed, as an item of consecutive prose— until now. Perhaps that reflects the fact that it cannot really be seen as a novel, but is more reminiscent of a literary collage lacking in form and conventional narrative; in terms of the psychological and esthetic insight that it offers into the writer's peculiar creativity, however, it is invaluable, especially with the supplementation of the exemplary texts juxtaposed with it herein. The prose poems are among the most extreme examples of the produce of the Decadent Movement, and the short novel is a fascinating commentary on the psychology and esthetics of that Movement, in its overlap with the French Occult Revival.

The translation of "Le Feu sacré" was made from the relevant copies of *L'Initiation* reproduced on the Traditional Martinist Order website at *martinists.org*. The translations from *Poèmes en prose* were made from the copy of the 1898 Léon Vanier edition reproduced on the Internet Archive Digital Library website at *archive.org*.

Brian Stableford

THE SACRED FIRE

I. The Temple

"There's a step," said Lucia.

She was standing on the threshold with a torch in her hand. The door was at the bottom of a slope on the side of the villa. The entire house, save for that retreat, was plunged in silence and obscurity. There was no silver stripe in the gaps of the shutters to divulge the interior life. A trellis embroidered with ivy surmounted the triangular wall near the door to the tunnel, and the moon, aided by the nocturnal breeze, made the sharp and dreamlike shadow of the foliage tremble on the white façade. Lucia's torch was also trembling, and paling in the pale air. The young woman, clad in a long black robe, evoked the image of welcome at the entrance to the catacombs. Saint-Maur saluted her with a smile over which a vertical finger put a cross of complicity. Then, making his companion the same sign to be quiet, he drew him inside.

There were ancient high-ceilinged cellars beneath the house. From outside, their existence could not be suspected, because the foundations of the house left no visible opening. Doubtless the ventilation of that part of the dwelling was enabled by secret passages, and lamps must burn there continuously. Such enclosed solitudes were found in the neighborhood of large cities, which served as the habitation of the mysteries. Every human city is ringed by houses for phantoms. With a divination of that vicinity, the dead too are sent into fraternal suburbs.

They were under the somber vault, and the door immediately closed behind them, as if invisible hands had been awaiting the signal. The two young men shivered at the sudden impact, but Lucia made a sign that they should follow her. Their silhouettes danced in the torchlight over their footsteps in the corridor, sometimes following them with the blackness of their movements, sometimes elongating over the vault, cut or twisted by the projection of a ledge. They passed several closed doors barred with iron, and two or three bays guarded by grilles, behind which stairways plunged into the darkness. At the turning of the steps down below, a nightlight fanned the walls with a dubious light. Then the route went round a bend, and Jean Derève perceived the entrance to a vaulted room, into which their guide introduced them. She designated seats next to a table surmounted by candelabra, and disappeared.

Once alone, the young men consulted one another with their gaze, exchanging mute impressions. The fashion in which they had been brought was strange. A carriage had awaited them at the exit from Saint-Maur's house, with a companion they recognized by means of words agreed in advance. They had been asked to permit their eyes to be blindfolded. That was the obligatory ceremony of excursions of this sort.

They remembered the vehicle going through the evening streets then, by roundabout routes deflecting all conjecture, and eventually rolling along a road that appeared to them to be outside the city, without them being able to determine in which direction they were going. A fleeting impression when they got down in front of the house and the blindfold had been removed had enabled them to suppose that they were at the end of some deserted avenue, near a wood. Perhaps all the twists and turns had not taken them very far, and the city was hiding close by, behind two or three curtains of trees.

They also knew that after their introduction, having made an oath of silence, they would be left at liberty to find the way back. That mystery, not of long duration, did not trouble them.

For the moment, they were solicited by the aspect of the place. They saw a kind of narrow cell, which must have been made for waiting, only furnished by dark wooden seats and a table. The walls, like those of the corridor, were made of stone separated by lines of cement; it was the décor of church walls and cloisters. That geometric disposition was the only ornamentation. They could have believed that they were in an Egyptian hypogeum, inhabited by a population of silent mummies gilded by immortality, or one of the chambers located inside pyramids, linked by long dark corridors, over which the mass of triangular granite weighs, while outside were clouds of sand stirred up by the desert wind, the sun and the cries of birds.

There are mysteries that requite lugubrious clearings in the forest, with the rustle of leaves and the pale face of Hecate through the black braches and the frightened howling of shepherds' dogs. Others are celebrated underground, fleeing the gaze of the blue sky, where the intermediation of gnomes or vagabond sylphs is invoked.

No rumor came from the rooms that must be nearby, separated from one another by the walls of the foundations. A few minutes went by. Jean Derève became discouraged. He had only accepted the initial precautions with great difficulty. An anxious desire had caused him, after successive vain experiments, to entrust himself to Saint-Maur. Like many others, he was in search of a formula for life, but his desire had become an impatience. Why were these delays and veils of ceremony always disposed at the entrance to the sanctuary? Would the truth not have gained from being shown suddenly, stark naked? The memory returned to his mind of other initiations whose exterior preparations had only been romantic jugglery devoid of purpose. He did not think that mystery belonged equally to the rites of wisdom and error. It was appropriate that different things had similar appearances, in order that one could employ reasoning.

"We have to resign ourselves," Saint-Maur said, "to finding veils everywhere. Isis is always under the mantle. You're complaining about a darkness whose contrast alone makes light. The High Priest of Jerusalem only entered the Holy of Holies once a year. It would not have been the Holy of Holies if the crowd had had the leisure to penetrate it every day. Think of the cavern of Arabian tales in which the precious gems and sacks of gold are heaped up, the door of which only opens to those who know the magic word.

"You think that deceptive forms have duped us too frequently by their appearances. A fine knight of adventures, truly, the man who is astonished to encounter enchantments, monsters and mirages in the forest, and who would like to see the hospitable threshold of the castle appear at the first bend, without going astray. You know that the chatelaine ought only to be smiling, that the pages ought only to be walking clad in gold and lace, and the brass trumpets ought only to be sounding to welcome the weary and sad visitor whose mantle is torn by all the thorn-bushes. But even if the ritual walls that loom up before you only have symbolic value, they must be accepted.

"The winner of the ancient games penetrated his natal city on his return by means of a breach made in the wall. Honor is signified by effort. Pythagoras spent thirty years in silence and study before being initiated into the Egyptian mysteries. All things differing, one can at least approve of the ceremonies that remind us of the difficulties. Anyway, I can hear voices through the thickness of the walls."

An invisible bay opened nearby, and Lucia returned. She was holding two red cloaks over her arm. The two companions put them on and followed her into the corridor. Other turnings, cleverly adapted into the restricted space of the subterrains, formed a veritable labyrinth, the extremity of which, for the range of voices and light, was a long way from the exterior. A corner crossed showed them, in a square niche in the wall, a statue that they recognized as that of Harpocrates, the god of silence.[4]

Lucia glided ahead of them; her black robe with moving pleats put bat-like shadows around her. One right-angled corridor was so narrow that they had to pass through it sideways one by one. It was a souvenir of epochs in which the research of obscure things had been regarded as a crime and the friends of the occult had been obliged to defend their dwelling. There are images that represent a vanished necessity. Events disappear but

---

[4] Harpocrates was a Greek adaptation of the Egyptian god Horus specific to Alexandria; that origin allowed his subsequent association by modern occultists with the supposed Gnostic phase of the Hermetic tradition.

forms endure. Many present rituals have that significance.

Lucia knocked on a door that was suddenly perceptible, which had a resonance of heavy wood. It swung on its hinges soundlessly, however. A bright light struck their faces, at the same time as perfumes and the sound of voices, and the visitors had the sanctuary before them.

It was a vast subterrain in the form of a hemicycle, with a much higher ceiling than the corridors. Only a few steps led to the lower level. The entrance on the threshold of which the young men were standing occupied the left of the diameter. They saw a bare room with the same regular design of stones. An odorous smoke blurred all the details. On each of the five arched walls with apparent ridges that formed the semicircle, wrought iron fittings bore yellow candles. Another, central light was coming from the long opposed wall; Saint-Maur and Derève supposed a hearth set back in its depth from the line.

In the low middle of the room, gray swirls of perfume were tinted with red light, rising like an exhalation toward the ceiling. The latter, posed over the bare walls, was painted pale blue, on which faint golden figures—lines, orbits and spheres—depicted the various systems of the world, with planets and comets, according to Copernicus, Ptolemy and the primitives. Around the subterrain men were standing clad in cloaks similar to those of the visitors, who remained on the threshold, somewhat nonplussed, awaiting a summons.

One member of the audience separated from the semicircle, conferred momentarily in a low voice with someone who could not be seen, hidden by a projection of the wall at the top of the staircase, and then came toward the young men. His face, like all the others, was almost entirely hidden by a vast hood, which the two newcomers did not have. There is no impression more anguishing than that of finding oneself with one's face uncovered, in a gathering of unknown and dissimulated persons.

The greeter, once having reached the highest step, said: "You do not know us, but we know you who you are. Before it is permitted for you to witness our sessions, swear to keep silent about everything you might hear and everything you might see. We shall leave you to return to our midst or to leave forever, as you wish. Everyone decides. But if you leave, you must forget, and never take the road that leads here with a profane. Make the oath.

"By what is it necessary to swear?" asked Saint-Maur.

"By the goddess."

They attested to the goddess that they would keep the secret.

The introducer took them by the hand and led them down the steps. Then they were taken to the center of the assembly. A man with his back turned to the hearth was in front of them, and in shadow, but the light was behind him, so he symbolized the obscure conductor toward it.

"What do you request?" he said. His voice was clear with a resonant timbre, enabling the supposition of a young man. His tone was reassuring.

Saint-Maur, instructed in advance, spoke first.

"We request the light."

The interrogator added: "What do you know?"

"Our ignorance," said Saint-Maur.

"You will still be ignorant, since you are human, and for humans, to understand is to be brought back to humanity. You will still see with your eyes and you will hear with your ears. No one can even conjecture what things are in themselves. In order to know them in their essence, it would be necessary to be at the center of everything and each individual thing in particular. Have you even penetrated the nature of your soul and its place in infinity? But there is no real center. The true world only exists in the vision of an intelligence; enable your mind to become a center. You will have found the absolute when you know that everything is relative and you know more relationships.

"Forms are held together and summon one another by a mysterious bond. The universe is like a sumptuous fabric. As soon as one seizes it, it unfurls entirely, embroidered with signs in gold and crimson. You will never lift, even in moments of ecstasy, the sacred veil of Isis, but you might surprise, at any moment, a different movement of the goddess and find her present everywhere. The name under which you worship the universal law is unimportant; it has no name and no face. The supreme thought that is manifest will only ever exist for you in its manifestations. The sole objective of science is to attain unity.

"The value of the word is purely that of a symbol. A sign of the identical unknown that we perceive in everything, it marks the front with a emblem that reminds us of that identity. Seek to know the laws, instead of asking in a puerile manner whether their creator exists, and under what form imitative of human form, and whether his name is Zeus or Jehovah. Astronomers know that it is only for us that the stars are named Aldebaran, Cassiopeia and Sirius.

"That is why you must refrain from mistaking the formula of our research for a reality. If anyone tells you that we worship fire, believe it, while not believing it.

You are in the sanctuary of the most ancient religion. It is the one from which all the others have come. They have preserved some of its rites, mingled with crude and new superstitions, but all flames and all candles are lit at the same altar. We have chosen the symbol that appears to us to be the most venerable and the best. In order to speak to humans it is necessary to speak human language. All things are signs, however, and signs of other signs. After having seen, you can only conjecture."

The man who had spoken appeared to be the high priest, or at least the initiator. When he fell silent, all the members of the audience sat down in chairs, the high backs of which bore figures engraved in the wood. They were arranged against the wall; the assembly thus formed the magical semicircle. The high priest occupied the center. The hearth was now visible in front of which he was standing: a vast niche hollowed out in the wall, arched in form, floored with paving stones, with a flue above it.

The flames of the burning wood, almost a furnace, shone violently, The pellicle of gray dust, the image of cooling stars, did not have time to form over the ardor of red embers. A perpetual breath of air stimulated them. To each side of the hearth, on the wall of the room, there were two fountains with the heads of chimeras in green bronze, to pour water into two round stone basins set on the floor. Everything seemed made to be interpreted.

The assembled audience no longer formed a perfect circle. That is a figure that represents the absolute, and the most fortunate image by which we can express our impotence to express it. However, like all definitions of the world or of God, it is a sterile formula. One cannot enclose being—or, to put it another way, becoming—within a closed line. Circumference indicates repose and

21

achievement. Life is movement and perpetual exchange. But the semicircle preserves the possibility of the beyond. It is continued by two parallel lines that extend into the distance and whose appeal is prolonged to the limits of supposed space. And if we are, in our inferior nature, the reflection of a higher nature, as Plato thought, the semicircle aspires to completion by another, actual or created by us, but situated in infinity. The focal point placed in its axis is also the reflection of another focal point.

Those thoughts were engendered, confusedly, in the minds of the visitors. They had the impression of living, momentarily, in a milieu haunted by symbols. But symbolism is all of literature, all of art and all of religion. It is the reduction of things to unity, the discovery of the same rhythm in the diversity of planes. Christ only spoke in parables, and everything is similar. The secrets of ancient science and magic are enveloped in legend, like transparent veils. Great poets are those who encounter unexpected and accurate images—which is to say, new relationships.

The décor differed here from the usual banality, or rather, it had the perfect banality that is a harmony. Only the red cloaks, the color of which was a natural concession in the sanctuary of fire, put a romantic note into that discreet concert. Jean Derève evoked other séances. He reviewed the various initiatory interiors previously traversed, in which the cult of Isis, as well as that of the Great Architect,[5] was adorned with faded garments and cabalistic figures in gilded cardboard. How many tem-

---

[5] The Great Architect (of the Universe) is the deity of freemasonry, within which tradition Martinism and modern Rosicrucianism evolved before separating therefrom.

ples had the sole aim of permitting the priests to live on the credulity of the fervent! He remembered naked swords crossed over the heads of the audacious, and Hebrew words pronounced on the threshold of equivocal sanctuaries by people so ignorant that they pronounced them purely because to them, they were Hebrew.

But perhaps, he thought, sadly, that was the foundation of everything, and images are always required to amuse the human child; the most delicate require more artistry in the line and the color.

Meanwhile, the high priest continued:

"Do not form a judgment of what you have seen before having meditated. All forms can only suggest, without representing, the unknown gods. The mages of all times have sought the unique principle. Some have believed that they had found it, and the result as the same, for the truth is revealed under one or other of its appearances to those who invoke it with a pious heart. There is no futile prayer, and sincere errors are errant on the route of the absolute. The act of faith to the veritable deity is composed of multiple invocations to all strange idols, and the name of the Supreme Being consists of the numerous syllables that denominate the numerous false gods. That is why, and to appease the secondary demons as well as the transitory powers, we have accepted as a departure the rite of the four elements. The quaternary is sacred. What does it matter whether we address our preliminary homage to mobile water, with Thales, to subtle air, with Anaximander, or to the earth, mother of humans, since everything is resolved in fire. Worship with us the four elements."

Immediately, the faithful rose to their feet and started to march around the room, stopping at the third circuit. One of them went into a neighboring room to fetch

23

a light column whose superior tablet was broad and covered by a black veil. The irregular pleats of the veil hid objects of worship.

"This black veil," said the High Priest, will be for you the somber chaos in which all the elements are buried. What a powerful hand it required to bring them out of primal chaos!"

He lifted the cloth, a cup appeared full of water, which was water, a vase full of salt, which was earth, and a rose, to signify the perfumes of the air.

Then everyone remained silent. The High Priest had thrown the veil into the hearth. The elements were created. The somber object flew away into the chimney like a crimson flag. There were a few minutes of slight anguish. Then, slowly, in the calm air, a voice rose that appeared to come from the depths of the earth. Afterwards the accompaniment of an organ also very distant, commenced. And, changing the words in a minor key, the subterranean voice pronounced the orison of the water elementals:

Masters of the ocean and all the shores
Who hold in power the moving ground of the waves,
Kings of caverns, the rain and clouds
Whom spring summons to the doors of enclosures,
You who come to open the source of springs,
And fecundate the bushes and the powerful oak,
Enabling to circulate in the network of veins
The limpid water changed into their sap and blood,
We here salute your magical power,
And your voice speaks to us with the sound of great waters,
But we also understand you in the music
Of the summer spring that cradles the birds.

Heights that reflect the profound immensity,
Depths that exhale you into the heights,
Give us the true sense of life and the world
In which eternal exchange is the true creator.
Pour into our hearts the love of sacrifice,
In order that, having become better and wiser,
For the divine redemption of error and vice,
We can offer you water, blood and tears.[6]

The voice fell silent. The hierophant took the cup and poured a few drops of the ground, in libation. The cup passed from hand to hand, until the last. It was replaced, empty, on the sacred column.

Meanwhile the organ rumbled, and the sanctuary was surrounded by a tumult similar to that of great waters. The voice rose up again, but it appeared to be coming from a profound retreat. It was the earth elementals that it invoked:

O you who haunt the human vault beneath our feet,
And make it tremble over its profound gulfs,
In the name of the seven torches of the sovereign
night
Lead us toward the light of which we dream.
Reveal to our eyes fixed on the mystery
The lost talismans of the holy city,
Which you keep hidden in the bosom of the earth

---

[6] The four parts of this invocation had previously appeared in the literary section of the November 1900 issue of *L'Initiation*. A similar ritual is described in Victor-Émile Michelet's "Holwennioul," published in his occult periodical *L'Humanité Nouvelle* in 1899, although that ritual also includes the swords treated dismissively here.

Under the seal of silence and obscurity.
Master of nocturnal laborers whose task
Is to reunite the gold of the dispersed veins,
As soon as we have labored relentlessly
With the sure hope of being recompensed,
Magnify our hearts for future labors,
You who inspire us with the occult and its desire,
And who wear, reigning over obscure splendors,
The sky on a finger, like a sapphire ring.

As he had done for the water, the priest lifted the
vase, took a grain of salt and placed it on his lips. The
members of the audience did likewise, and the voice
continued, imploring the elementals of the air:

You whose breath creates and destroys all form,
Spirit who travels borne on the wings of the wind,
Your respiration populates enormous space,
Life is like a shadow to your moving gaze.
You guide, alternated beneath a magical power,
The ravens of night and the doves of day,
Enable, with the light of your mystic soul,
The breath of amour to penetrate our depths.
One day, to the eternal movements of this world
All wanderers will be encountered by others,
And, dreams mutated into profound verity,
Roses will grow on the branches of cypresses.
Like shipwreck victims battered by the tempest,
We are struggling in the horror and error of dusk,
But our hearts have known the preparatory calm,
And the dawn is as odorous as a censer.
Vast sigh that silenced the ancient creator,
Mouth of shadow exhaling the eternal mystery,
By means of perfumes, colors and music,

Baptize us in the subtle and fraternal air.

Everyone respired the rose. The sacred objects were taken away; the assembly formed the circle again and, all is members prostrate, listened to the orison of the salamanders, the demons of the inferior fire.

Eternal, uncreated Father of all things,
Whose triumphal chariot rolls over the world,
Real fire of Eternity, Cause of causes,
Inspire us with the prayers to be offered to you.
The throne where you sit dominates the expanse,
Nothing escapes the immense gaze of your eyes.
Every word pronounced is heard.
Grant our prayers, you who hide behind the gods!
Compared with your splendor, the stars are mere
ash,
You shine in the height of the sky as within us,
Into our obscurity deign to send down
The light of which the suns are jealous.
Reign over us by means of heat and light,
Cold shadow is the mortal sister of the void,
Every ray surging from the primal source
Creates a new world in the gaping abyss.
We know that from your unique power are born
Souls, desire and amour, the golden torch,
Beneath the vain formula and the ancient image,
It is always you that humans have adored.
All the sacred mantles are only shrouds
In which resuscitate form and the only God,
And lamps are on the threshold of various sanctuar-
ies,
As witnesses of the true worship, that of fire.

For it was appropriate to invoke the supreme element with more solemnity, and to implore it first in its humblest manifestation. Terrestrial and perishable fire, to the surveillance of which the salamanders are appointed, is only the least reflection, in the distant obscurity, of the immortal and primitive fire. The latter respires the infinite. On the road that leads to it, as the highest image visible for us, is the Sun.

And that was the prayer to fire. The same servant stood up, and went to take from a cupboard firmed by a hollow in the wall, a red book, which he brought piously to the middle of the room.

He deposited it on a light and high table and opened it. The letters were black, arched in form. The yellow paper was tinted with nuances in which the appearances of smoke and flame were recognizable. The reader chanted:

"I salute you, Ignis, Agni, lamb of fire, Ormuz. Osiris, Mithra, who are manifest by way of Yama, the thunder, and by way of Athene, the lightning. Father of Phobos and Hephaestos, it is to you alone, under various names, that humans render homage, to you alone, O our god."

A response ran through the religiously attentive audience:

"*Soli deo, deo soli!*"

"I salute you, you who are born and die at the solstice and emerge from the sepulcher on the third day, Adonis, Adonai, Jesus, god of the pyre and the cross. Merciful and cruel God, Moloch requiring victims, brazen bull with ardent flanks, eye that shines at the center of the triangle and flame that it summarizes, angel that appeared in the bush. I shall turn my gaze toward the Orient, where you triumph incessantly, and from which you rise toward the zenith, to succumb in the Occident. By your fall, the glorious sea is illuminated in its depths. The glaucous and somber populations that its abysms contain, have your revelation every evening. On your sparkling tracks people and humanity go.

"I shall turn my eyes toward the Occident where you flee in order to carry life beyond. The watchers look out for your approach, and the mountains are crowned by temples consecrated to you, O Helios, Saint Hélie.[7] Rising sun, surrounded by a cortege of hours in roseate robes, pouring flowers of joy from their hands. Flame of the heart above the earth, lightning-flash, star in the sky, fire that consumes offerings and divine fire that receives them, shadow of the ineffable cause, blinding for mortal eyes, you who are born of two mothers and who have your cradle for a tomb, it is in you alone that we ought to believe and to whom we should sacrifice; to you alone, O solar god!"

The voice of the recitation was impregnated with fervor. Then it fell silent.

Perfumes poured from bronze cups over the red embers emerged slowly in dense white swirls of smoke, toward the vault, like the columns of an unreal temple.

A different voice continued:

"And I salute you also, among humans, the discoverer of fire, Prometheus!

"What unjust forgetfulness spreads its shroud over you, father and creator?

---

[7] The reference is not to Saint Hélie of Lyon, but rather to the Abrahamic prophet usually known in English as Elijah, sometimes called Élie or Hélie in French; the author prefers the latter term in order to forge the link with Helios.

"It was a crime to want to posses the god, Had he truly made humans in an hour of wrath, that he was irritated by your theft? But bow down before his jealous fury, for he has allowed you to keep the shreds of the mantle, crimson and gold, that you stole. Everything that he wants is just and good. He has not chained you to your rock for eternity. The thrust of the sword causes a spark to spring from the rock, and you climb up again toward he gods to perpetuate your memory by means of the lamps that watch over the various altars. True Adam, you rediscovered the sacred fire lost by the first Adam. It is your story that all the sibylline books contain.

"O Prometheus!

"We have been the slaves of the clouds and the wind. Do you recall human life before the invention of fire. But he came to soften the curbed forms of iron for weapons and the plow. The earth gave wheat. Flame hollowed out trees and the first ship floated. Let it cry humankind! It conquered the face of night. When the god disappeared in the decreasing crimson of the horizon, having become blue again, instead of invoking the pale moon or obscure goddesses by means of incantations, we stimulated, in order to render homage to him, the shining shadows of the sun.

"Lamp!

"Vacillating torch of the miner who plunges, by way of sloping subterrains, into the region of heavy air.

"Lamp of the laborer curbed by night over the blank sheet or the page of a book; the light is in his soul as well as around him.

"Lamp of amour that fearful Psyche approached to the unknown!

"Spark come from above, what poet of works in the fabulous vanished night pronounced the breathless emotion of the first undulation of your blue flame?

"Glimmers of summer hidden in the hollows of old trees, from which we make them surge forth, like ancient shepherds, by striking two white stones, enabling the nymph with the golden hair to appear from the centenarian oak.

"Take homages in your hands, like garlands of red roses, and rise again toward the solar god."

Silence reigned again; but it was troubled. Indistinct noises were coming from the door. Moans and sobs were heard. All of them directed their gazes toward...

"The adoration of fire," said a voice.

The perfumes of cups flowered myrrh and aloes. An odorous smoke misted the room and oppressed hearts. The torches gleamed beneath a veil. A religious torpor almost suffocated the members of the audience, and in the atmosphere, in which red and fleeting gleams enlaced, fatigued eyes were ready to see the strangest forms, by means of the fantasy of evocation.

Meanwhile, the sobs continued on the other side of the wall. They were mingled with ecstatic plaints. A new pity seemed to be begging to be received. The High Priest headed toward the entrance and the visitor.

The door opened, and a man appeared: an old man with twisted limbs, a grimacing face furrowed by deep wrinkles, he evoked the supreme limits of age. His appearance was sudden and bizarre. A black robe with wide sleeves, secured at the waist by a rope, dressed ineptly a dwarfish and disproportionate body, with an enormous had covered in gray hair. One might have thought, on seeing the gaze of his green eyes, that he was a veritable gnome emerged from some fantastic realm. It is certain that envoys from the neighboring world live among us. The entire person of the old man inspired alarm.

He was seen to descend the steps jerkily, hopping from one foot to the other. He could not aid himself with the walls. His hands were hidden over his breast by a flap of his robe. With crawling movements, turning from one side to the other, he came all the way to the middle of the room. Each of his movements was accompanied by the same sobs, marks of madness of emotion. Suddenly, however, having reached the center of the curved line formed by the initiates, as if at a real focal point, he straightened up and was almost august. His arms were disengaged from the folds of the robs, and the young men perceived a small object shining on his hands, raised and joined.

In the midst of bewildered starts and acclamations, Jean Derève, aided by his companion's smile, sensed present impressions fusing with a vanished memory. He knew the talisman that the clenched fingers were holding aloft. Curious about occult things, he had been amused by the story, as a poetic legend; but he had to believe it now.

No jewel approaches for beauty a fragment of an ardent furnace. Red is the color of blood and life; but precious stones are like dead beauties. If fire did not pale and fall into ash, if it could remain as it is in the heart of a hearth it would be the most splendid of rubies. No rajah of fabulous India possess anything similar in his treasures. Tradition requires the existence of that impossible jewel to be accepted.

A mineral whose nature could not be precisely determined served as a pretext for all that worship, and its mysterious nature was not in contradiction with the new suppositions that stupefied science sees realized every day. The properties of substances differ. That means that each contains and reveals a form of energy. Some are luminous. Others can, with brightness, produce a constant heat. In the midst of adorations and ritual precautions, they kept the fiery stone discovered by a Bohemian, whom the poetic imagination had made into a messenger of the sun. For, with the brightness of the most beautiful rubies, it was also a perpetual ardent coal. It burned without being consumed, and it redness, which passed from vivid to dark, for the various joy of the eyes, was not a deceptive symbol. Visible Fire, at its approach all hands, including those of the most pious, became profane. One could no more grasp it than a firebrand. It was intangible, like flame, lightning and mystery. That is a religious quality, for our corporeal person. And certainly, with the love of the extraordinary that is human, such an object can sustain astonishment better that fetishes of wood or stone. It has not always required as much for people to make a god.

It could be compared to the philosopher's stone, or the ember placed by an angel on the lips of Moses. According to the legend, the talisman had been conserved in a sanctuary in India, sheltered in a hollow granite container sculpted in a triangular form to signify the pure fire represented by the pyramids, and then, after several voyages, transported to Europe. A faithful follower, doubtless one of the last descendants of Asiatic worshipers, a guardian of the occult tradition, jealous of exposing it to the gaze of his brethren and of making it the occasion of ceremonies, had undertaken to set the jewel in a metal bezel. It is appropriate that every idol can be presented by the priest above the prostrate crowd, to receive prayers and vows. The discovery of a metal capable of retaining the stone without being damaged by the contact had demanded patience and an entire lifetime. Now, the man to whom its pious care was entrusted elevated in his hands a light reliquary, from the heart of which it cast its durable fires around. But by virtue of keeping the talisman captive in its metal circle during the hours of religious penalty, the hands of the worker, gloriously burned, were deformed and mutilated. It was said that they could no longer serve any other purpose than holding the reliquary in a definitive grip. Black and twisted, they retained the indestructible marks of the wounds made by the god.

Meanwhile, the uninterrupted groans of the old man were mingled with the invocations of the entire audience. Some, standing in various parts of the room, in ecstatic poses, seemed to be challenging the idol. Others, fallen to their knees, their heads buried under their cloaks, were sobbing hectically. Appeals in all languages were overlapping, for there were doubtless initiates in the modern city who had come from the most diverse regions, united by a common faith.

The scene became tragic. The red smoke undulated, making bodies appear, at the whim of the flames, in strange attitudes, like the forms that one dreams for a subterranean inferno. The High Priest remained motionless, sitting in his chair in the middle of that human swell, his eyes on the stone and the old man. He represented, in a fleeting vision, the bleak master of the Sabbat seen in ancient prints, his hand on his chin and his elbow on his knee.

The young men, nonplussed, and understanding that those men were unaware henceforth of the presence of strangers, feared some unexpected development. As they took refuge by the door, it opened slightly, and the silhouette of Lucia made a shadow. She beckoned to them from outside.

When they were in the vestibule, she closed the door behind them, through which clamors were now audible. They traversed the narrow and winding passages again. Jean Derève and Saint-Maur reached the room where they deposited their red cloaks. Then Lucia conducted them, in the diminishing echo of distant voices, to the external threshold.

She saluted them with a smile and he same gesture of silence. They had the bewilderment of a sudden contrast. Trees of all shades of green were agitating in the breeze. The sun was nascent in its freshness, and there was a slight joy in respiring, while mist was rising from the landscape in order to vanish impalpably, like another incense, toward the red disk on the horizon.

II. Counsel

The apartment that Jean Derève inhabited was in a peaceful street. It was furnished with books, candles and comfortable chairs, more appropriate to dreaming than work. Bright tapestries covered the walls, where no painting could be seen. Perhaps precise images, placed eternally before he eyes, take fantasy prisoner in a redoubtable fashion. Those whom lines oppress avoid the continual vision of the same design. Any excessively present form invades and tyrannizes them. At least, if one has to resign oneself to living surrounded by suggestion, it is necessary for it to be exquisite. For want of liberty one accepts a gilded slavery. Such individuals would allow themselves to be influenced, in accordance with the state of the soul, by Boucher, Goya or Leonardo da Vinci. But the mediocrity of contemporary existence only permits that luxury to a few privileged people, whom other necessary concerns prevent them from enjoying it.

And if paintings are a shadow of the real, reproductions or copies are the shadow of a shadow; the charm does not go as far. It is necessary not to talk about vulgar things. One can accept facing one, for minutes of repose, the domination on the wall of a virgin with a chaste gaze, or, at the top of a column, the haunting of a bacchante with a beautiful body. It is sad to raise one's submissive eyes toward a caricature or an inharmonious contour. The only décor for the modest artist ought to be superimposed on a bare panel, which he populates with fearful figures or landscapes, at his whim. Two or three ornamental mirrors also introduce the beyond. Gilded frames are the same.

Mirrors open, it is true, a bizarre door to the unknown. One dare not look at them too closely when one is alone, for fear of perceiving that one is no longer alone. Astral larvae take refuge on the other side of the wall in an unreal apartment that reproduces, with a slightly satanic exactitude, since it is reversed, all the details of this one. What apprehension there is of perceiving, in the tilted light of candles, a face other than our own! How necessary it is to be attentive to taking the necessary precautions!

The invisible invades us through all open windows. One can utilize magic mirrors to communicate at a distance, but the bright glasses are haunted. It is better to suppose that the golden frame is the same as that, and cause to pass into the apartment a happy silhouette of a living woman. Every mirror before which her grace moves becomes, by receiving it in passing, the fugitive masterpiece of an unknown painter.

Saint-Maur and Jean Derève were sitting beside a blazing fire, by which the rather cold morning was being warmed. The shadows of the flames were dancing on the ceiling, like weightless black dancers. Both of them, in the intervals of a slow conversation, were staring at the hearth, where heaped up red embers were erecting bizarre architectures. At other times they designed figures at a stroke, a contest of scattered and grimacing gnomes was suddenly changed into something new by the collapse of firebrands. It is not astonishing that divination by fire is a common practice. All humans observe the marvelous things that are discovered there. Better than on the plaster of old walls, with more intense color and relief, one can create in flame the forms that one wants.

"Are you not thinking," said Saint-Maur, "of becoming one of the prophets that praise the cult of fire? What memory have you retained, and what impression, of your visit? You're looking toward the fireplace with the air of an initiator."

His friend shook his head. "It would be necessary, in order for me to persuade others, to be convinced myself. But I'd be a poor hierophant, stammering the sacred words with a timid mouth and an unsure heart. Then again, everyone ought to be his own initiator. The most savant can only advise us to lend an ear to the voice that speaks within us. However, I thank you for having enabled me to penetrate a mysterious circle. One isn't obliged to believe in order to admire the faith of others, and I think that it's necessary to multiply experiments in order to find the truth one day. But I'm a skeptical seeker, and, like the Hermotimus of the admirable Lucian,[8] I'm afraid of not being able to reach the summit of the mountain. That's a great pity. It would please me to know what temple stands there, and what definitive god manipulates the lightning. For want of that, my nonchalance willingly arrests its step on the threshold of some sanctuary half way up, with flute-players and the shade of trees near a spring. But Epicureans are poor folk. They're the voluntary vanquished enlacing their chains

---

[8] The reference is to a dialogue by Lucian known in English as *Hermotimus; or, The Rival Philosophers*. The eponymous character is based on Hermotimus of Clazomenae, described by Lucian as a Pythagorean philosopher, although other accounts have Pythagoras claiming Hermotimus as one of his previous incarnations; he is usually cited as a dualist who distinguished between mind and matter and represented mind as the agent of all change.

of flowers. Facile joy appears to me to be difficult to accept. A pretentious man, I want happiness. Ordinary and calm life, deprived of anxiety, isn't sufficient to content me. Tell me, you whom I suppose to be a master in the meritorious art of regulating his opinions and his life, what is it necessary to believe in order to be happy?"

"In everything and nothing."

"An admirable response, of which I suspect, without being sure of it, the profound meaning. Perhaps, remaining in the domain of rationality, you mean that everything is true, and that different theories are only different points of view. Is it, on the contrary, a practical advice? Is it a matter of arriving at the bizarre state in which the soul, understanding more and more, loses the faculty of being moved? Let's admit that that is the objective. I have the apprehension of a desolating verity, which experience has confirmed for me. Everything that is desirable is only beautiful before being possessed. It's not a new idea, but we don't do anything, between birth and death, except accept proverbs at first, and perceive afterwards, in the course of experience, their sudden exactitude and their real meaning.

"The poor fellow who envies riches doesn't realize that, if he made a fortune, he would no longer see it with the eyes of a poor man but those of the opulent man that he would then have become. It would be necessary, absurdly, to possess things with the soul of someone who does not possess them. The saints have realized that antinomy, but it is another sense. Our joy no longer depends on gazing, in a fashion as melancholy as it is happy, at that of which we have become the masters. To possess is to dominate, to be beyond desire. And the felicity that I seek is, once found, no longer felicity."

"It isn't demonstrated," said Saint-Maur, "that the goal of life is happiness, or, at least, that there is only one happiness. You're supposing in all men, for the sake of simplification, the same aspirations as there are in you, and the same impotence to realize an appropriate form of existence. But to begin with, the disposition of which you're complaining is exceptional; and in addition, one has to know how to take advantage of it. There are various dwellings in the temple of wisdom. The progress of individuals is as personal as their gait.

"Some people adopt definitive gestures in adolescence, slowly but surely. They accustom themselves, after every stage, to the necessary changes. They are like travelers sitting in an inn, under the shade of a tree, saying to themselves that they have come from elsewhere, and are going elsewhere. The time of the relay is broadly sufficient; the horses are changed, and the postillion goes to drink.

"Our travelers know the future halts. They know that at such an age, they will have a particular speech, a particular attitude, and a particular vain assurance in discussions. None of them senses anxiety, at the approach of maturity, of one day evoking white horses or comparing present impressions with those once experienced in childhood, feeling astonishment and anguish at what has disappeared. They are the placid and banal herd, marching after the hour as if behind a known herdsman. Successively, they accept to don the various costumes and appear in the next act with the role known and the appropriate mask. Thus, in ancient plays the actor puts on the face of an old man in the final scenes.

"But for others, what a difference there is! Their days follow one another too rapidly. Scarcely have they seen the sunrise than they are already afraid of the night.

By a strange contrast, their childhood lasts longer. They always experience the same surprises, and the quotidian repetition of the spectacle does not blunt their senses. On the contrary, their soul emerges from each of those encounters as if from a cold bath, which renders it more capable of shivering. They only have to think that a mystery is incomprehensible to renew it at every heartbeat of life, no less incomprehensible. They are eternal children. The others, so promptly habituated and reasonable, are born old. And truly, in spite of the universal bitterness, isn't it better to see existence as a tableau that is always unexpected? Is not the only achievable happiness always to have eyes for which everything is new, and lips for which every kiss is the first?

"I'm only talking about the latter people. They have, to the highest degree, the faculty of realizing a more desirable vision, if they wish it. For the only art is the art of living. You lament possession, and expectation seems to you to be better. Effort appears futile to you, for the result would disenchant you, because you do not know that the joy is in the effort. Have you never had the pride of striving, and that of succeeding? The development of activity bears its recompense within itself. It is necessary to march toward the goal in order to attain it, but above all to take account of the fact that one can march. The rest is only a slight recompense, like crowns of foliage. The essential thing is to have been manifest.

"Those people who create dreams, in order to express them in music, words or color, are only projecting their internal impressions outside themselves. They are thoughts issued from their bodies, like phantoms, which wander like Egyptian doubles through the vast world. They are exposed to encounters, sometimes exquisite, of which their creators are almost always ignorant. He lives

41

within them, however, and ordinarily cares little about the art in his own life.

"But the true visionary does not think of writing poems or tracing colored lines. An unusual spectacle unfurls before his eyes. A play that is by turns a pantomime, a drama, a comic opera or a legend, is performed for him. He is like a prince of Bavaria sitting, bleak and alone, in the hall of a dimly lit theater. He can only confide his trouble, after a tragic scene, or his joy when the young man in love sings marvelously, to phantoms whispering behind the empty armchairs or leaning out, laughing, from the gaping boxes. Behind the doors and in the corridors, the servants are waiting, and the courtesans, who are honored by a key embroidered on the back, putting their ear to them in order to hear a fragment of the play, or an eye, in order to catch a furtive glimpse of their beloved prince. They do not hear any of the words or any of the music, and the prince remains alone.

"But I would rather be, instead of that pure contemplator, someone who is able to create for himself the spectacle that amuses him. The dreamer is at the mercy of his sensibility, if he is not able to direct it. Let him be a willful philosopher, for the value of a man is measured by his will. That is the only god, the mobile god. When it is not the brute force of a conqueror or a courier, but is accompanied by intelligence, a man becomes capable of guiding his own prayers. He is the master of existence and he composes, with his actions, his emotions and his attitudes, a poem having the strange superiority of being alive.

"How many people you know who complain of never having known happiness or certainty! That is because they have waited for happiness under the elm tree instead of marching straight ahead and creating it by marching. One often perceives too late that we only receive at birth the raw material of our existence. It is for us to give it form, to learn that a block of wax has been set before us that is equal for all; but some shred the block of wax, or abandon it idly; others model it patiently, and under their charmed fingers see a vase with delicate lines blossom, or a beautiful statue. We are the ones who fashion our lives, and we can make a masterpiece if we wish. But how many, by virtue of nonchalance, are divine hours unrealized!

"One should not be discouraged, however All men do not take possession of themselves at the same moment. There are some who know with certainty, from the first day, what they want. In others, the personality is slower to become distinct. They know themselves later. I would willingly believe that the law of progress is the same everywhere. The man who only arrives at being himself after long years can conjecture that his life will be longer. The mid-point of existence is not the same for all. A belated youth accords poorly with a premature old age. We are like plants to some extent. An oak is still nascent and frail while a bush had finished its days. So do not lament not having yet arrived at the moment of knowledge and anxiety. You will live to be very old. But it's necessary not to waste time."

"Will power," said Jean Derève, "is perhaps not equal in everyone. I find it just that the active alone possess the realm juxtaposed with that of god, which only belongs to the patient. That the intelligent man is never completely idle, I also grant. But some have a better share. Does the flame that burns in souls always have the same ardor?"

"I could respond to you," replied Saint-Maur, "that your difference does not matter; it would be sufficient if everyone realized his potential. You would not ask a sparrow to fly as high as an eagle. The bee, its hive constructed, has the right to be as proud as the architect who built to temple of Ephesus. Everyone does his best if he attains his ideal. That response would not satisfy me. It's a matter of analogous beings, able to pretend to an equal happiness, only differing in energy. The word 'potential' has two meanings; it designates both the ensemble of the faculties, and more especially, the art of developing them.

"Remember that, of all the faculties, the will is the most capable of education. There is no initiation that does not repose on that principle. If feeble, it can be fortified, and if false, corrected. One has the choice of willing, or abandoning oneself to the days that pass by, like a wisp of straw to the current of a river. Let us not reason like the wisp of straw. Very different means exist in order to affirm the hesitant personality and to permit it to know in what direction to go. The routes are numerous. But remember that the principal part of the voyage is the decision to make the voyage, and knowing that it is necessary to depart. The rest is an affair of indicators.

"Note that I'm a Platonist. To know the good and to decide to accomplish it are the same thing. It's already a great deal to take pleasure in the exercise of the will, and to treat it as a game. Be sure that, by virtue of an evident and understandable interest, we will direct the game in the most favorable fashion. One quickly perceives, once one pays attention, the unsuspected resources one possesses. The pleasure of that recognition is infinite; we are all, more or less, like childish magicians, who amuse themselves with the magic wand, or abandon it idly because they haven't yet discovered its charming virtue.

"Those whose energy is insufficient make appeal to stimulants. List the drugs and the poisons; the effects are different but the impulsion communicated is the same. We feel decreasing within us, by the hour, the vital force indispensable to the development of our self. Or, if the case presents itself, we are born with an atony that lowers all our manifestations. Then the role of the artificial intervenes. It's a delicate determination. The deplorable or beneficial results depend on the proportions. Voltaire drank seventy-four cups of coffee a day.[9] That excitation was necessary but exaggerated. It is permissible to explain thereby his cold fury and his unnatural talent.

"A good pharmacopeia would be a useful book, which will not be written. At any rate, the author will not be a physician, for physicians have the concern of making human life last, and not that of utilizing it. The secret harmonies between nature and man are scarcely suspected, and that it is possible to borrow fluid from the inferior world in order to rise to the one on high. Vegetables nourish the substance of flesh, their essences the astral body. To discus similar theories seriously, it is evident that one would be taken for a madman. That is in the order of things; it was always thus. And yet I must believe that in the absorption of elixirs or extracts, it is the soul of the plant that pass into us and sometimes astonishes us. The spiritual blood is formed by the same alchemy as the corporeal. The exact study of these phe-

---

[9] Most sources suggest that Voltaire only drank fifty cups of coffee a day, but some compensate by alleging that he put seven sugar-lumps in each one. The accounts are probably exaggerated.

nomena and their laws is an integral part of magic, which is itself, in its entirety, only the science of the will."

"Do you not think," Jean Derève objected, "that there are other methods for action? I praise those who make a game of developing their will. I understand, without approving of them, those who demand the necessary inspiration from accursed beverages. There are, however nobler philters: ambition, amour, and devotion. What a power an idea has! The great wills are those who march in pursuit of their dream, in the absolute joy and confidence that they are marching toward the truth. A route does not exist without a goal. For my part, I have always regretted not having had a belief, whatever it might be, and I've made every effort to accept the wager that the Jansenists inspired in Pascal. Vain efforts! What does it matter to me whether a doctrine is advantageous to follow? The only thing that I demand is that it should be true. With ardor, convinced, I would be devout. But the days are uniform and devoid of any pretext or heroism. The time has come, however, when I ought to commence living, if I don't want to die without having lived. I'm at the terrible age of a man. That of a woman is every day. Now, one is a young man, but one is no longer a young man, while awaiting the time when one becomes a man still young, which is the end of everything.

"If I return to hours presently elapsed, not only have I done nothing, which hardly matters, in terms of the importance of my feeble lost effort to humankind, but I have not been able to be happy, and that alone is important. I've allowed myself to drift along, as if on a changing wave. How many joys I have let pass unknowingly! Purely sensual joys, for the most part. They are the ones I regret the most. Smiling faces torture me in the past. And I review my existence as a dreary panto-mime played in successive décors.

"The cities!

"The first is an old Saracen city enclosed by ram-parts. People were massacred there once, in the name of fatherlands and religions, but today the round-paths are planted with fine idle plane trees. The narrow and wind-ing streets snake toward the old cathedral. There are black statues and grilled chapels in the walls at intersec-tions. The house was at the back of the courtyard. I lived my first hours there, an eternity. What an image for fu-ture visions, the first house! The broad staircase had an iron handrail. And my memory, climbing, stops in the middle of that stairway. A large tree on the façade next to a stone bench. The tree was felled before I left. On the other side of the house, the garden, narrow and sad. A door with have bars opened on the lateral street. It was there that I constructed the frame for all my dreams to come, and I knew emotions whose memory still fright-ens me today. I can hear, when I meditate, the sound of bells in the afternoon, and I see people in Sunday cloth-ing, their gilded book in hand, heading toward the portal for vespers.

"The other city was on the bank of a great river, from which mist rose all winter long, scarcely allowing the yellow halo of the street-lights to be divined. On the boulevard, in the fog, a carriage rolls. Ah, there's the merchant of images. The shop-front is closed. A balcony and its wrought iron recall to mind, for no reason, a morning in March.

"The hand of a tall person holds mine from above. The dull shops of narrower streets announce the quay. There are pulleys there above large bays in the wall. The

47

ground is slippery and black. Then the river, with its living banks. Sunlight traverses the mist. Sailors from far away are smoking short sculpted pipes. The yardarms of ships are swaying horizontally. My foot collides with heavy rings sealed in the paving-stones. I'm already thinking about voyages I shall never make, to calm and distant lands that I shall never visit.

"The last is a populous city on the edge of the sea, with colors and joy of which I'm ignorant. I've grown. I'm at the odious or divine age of adolescence, odious for me. The spontaneous and charming soul that was mine has been killed by a bad education. Vulgar men have taught me about life with formulae they don't understand themselves. I don't know the route to follow toward happiness, and I'm in a pitiful anguish. But I'll emerge from the tomb.

"Virtual impressions merit survival. There was the sea and the beach, where I know very well that I'll return when I'm weary of things. All of that flees like a distant vision, which reminds me nevertheless of having been so present. Existence is a mad game.

"Now, and a long time ago, I've arrived in the city with the beautiful river bordered by ramparts. I suspect realities the ignorance of which made all my misfortune; and I search recklessly, wanting to live, while there is still time, the formula of life."

Saint-Maur smiled. "You'll find it. It's useful to have lived in order to know. It's only by multiple experience that one arrives at unity. You understand that things have no value in themselves that merits our being moved by them, and that the vision is everything. There is nothing absolute, but only relativities. The present environment doubtless seems to you the most favorable to create your harmony; I agree to that. But everything

48

depends on that harmony. Only your soul is real, and the rest should only exist in accordance with your will. Don't believe that the world is such that it will reveal itself, and do so necessarily.

"It requires so little to overturn an ensemble that appears usual to us. Human life is the same in different centuries because the differences are irrelevant. One eats, one sleeps, one loves, one disputes positions, there are rich and poor, merchants, advocates and brothel-keepers today, exactly as in the epoch of Ramses or Nero. We live following custom and we place our feet in the tracks left by those who preceded us, like ancient carts passing through the streets in granite ruts. But make that dream of humankind different from ours in one essential detail, and see what follows from it, and everything will be changed.

Suppose that the habit has been acquired, which can be supposed, of living by night instead of by day. Nothing in civilization would be similar to that which is. Some people, it is true, realize that existence in part, and go to bed at the hour when others are getting up. But that is only an exception, which is discredited by the idea of the abnormal. We have all had the notion, going home at dawn after some night out, that our passage through the sad bands of street-sweepers and hasty workers was furtive and shameful. Already, however, it appears permissible, as the lighting improves, to prolong evenings. Thinkers like the silence that falls around their late vigils as the city sleeps. And it isn't only for pleasure and folly that the lamps are lit. There's a progress over ancient times, when people went to sleep with the daylight. One could plausibly sustain the paradox that intellectual illumination become brighter as others do. The number of lamps and their brightness is not indifferent in the judgment one makes of the mental value of a people.

"I don't want to follow that reasoning any further, nor what it would be possible to deduce from the sun actually disappearing, for that would be admitting the end of everything. We'll keep the pure hypothesis of a humankind living by night and going to sleep by day, in accordance with established principles. I'll gladly accept some religious reason: a people worshiping the sun, believing it to be sacrilege to confront it. Dusk would be the dark dawn when the earth would wake up, substituting one angelus for the other. The gleams of morning would be welcome to the eyes of the weary worker. The hours of toil and pleasure would be exchanged, and lovers would be seen addressing aubades to the sunlight. One would only consider important everything that is nocturnal. The art of illumination would become the foremost of all. It would be necessary, in fact, not to count on the stars or the moon, at the mercy of clouds and the time of year. Only sometimes, too infrequently for popular joy, would a beautiful clear night enable strollers to spread out into the country. But I can see silent men wandering through somber streets at sparkling crossroads. Prodigious searchlights pour their oblique white radiance over distant houses. Perhaps the passers-by have black garments. Perhaps they will seek to vanquish the surrounding obscurity by mans of the splendor of fabrics; but certain colors no longer exist, and the existence of a color is among the essential things.

"What new and sad idylls there would be on the banks of covered springs or in the profundity of woods! The laborer going by lantern-light to sow the wheat in the furrows would give the impression of accomplishing a funereal rite. Joy would no longer be that of today, for, undoubtedly, the soul would change. Expect new virtues and sins. It would be thought just to stone and crucify a man who had gone to pick a rose in broad daylight. Today the act of amour is a shameful crime; the incoherence is the same and the two ideas equivalent. Stupidity would have other gestures, but the number of errors would be similar. Perhaps, too, humankind would have taken a giant step on the road of progress. It would not have approached the goal; possibility is unlimited, but we would see strange things. Conjectures are amusing, and prove the relativity of things.

"You live, therefore, in the environment of a world that does not have a necessary form, and could be different. That is because its appearance depends on chance and circumstance, and has nothing essential about it. You could already have found calm by accepting to be the dilettante who smiles and passes by, and does not allow himself to be moved.

"The observation can also lead you to higher visions, if you imagine that beneath crazy appearances immutable laws persist, which are manifest in every fashion. The human race about which I was speaking just now would operate in a strangely different frame, but its primitive ideas would not have changed and its passions would be human. Under the most distant forms, existence is identical, and is only relative to the absolute, which is in our thought. All laws come back to the unique, well or poorly interpreted. You can construct your life according to your form. If you knew the law, you would be similar to the gods, because you would be able to create at will the world in which you ought to live.

"I'm sure that a magic word exists, a formula of philosophical transmutation, a key to the obscure science. The sphinx that the immortal Oedipus encounters in successive stages has the same smile in its gaze and maintains the same verbal silence. What is it, and what walls will fall when it is pronounced on the threshold of the treasure? Those who seek it in books will never find it, while the children of insouciant women pronounce it and do not recognize it. Let me remind you of a legend that you have already read. It has several meanings and several morals, which are closely connected. Its symbolism is very extensive. Suppose that I'm telling it solely for the pleasure of telling it.

"An old king has just died. His reign was celebrated throughout Asia, for he governed his people with prudence and authority. And in dying, he left a vast library, the largest that had ever been seen, doubtless similar to the one that the mariner in the Arabian Nights discovered under the mysterious mountain, and which torches illuminate from the end of one year to the next. The hereditary price mounted the throne and he was frightened, for he had no keener desire than to possess knowledge, and conjectured that it must be entirely contained in the library. He had no doubt that his father had extracted the secret of wisdom and happiness therefrom. It would therefore be desirable to read them all in order to have an entire knowledge, but the days of ten centuries would not be sufficient. How, on the other hand, could a choice be made? He suspected that, if he left one work aside, it would be precisely the one containing the indispensable principles and the most useful verities. The prime minister was summoned to give him advice. He was an old man with a white beard. He shook his head.

"'Sire,' he said, 'when His Majesty your father invested his confidence in me, I was a poor shepherd. One day, the king had gone astray after a hunt. He asked me for directions, and I made him responses that permitted him to suppose that I was a man of good sense. He appointed me as his prime minister, as you have heard it said that he once did. I have scarcely found time since then to complete my instruction. I know how to reprimand a steward who steals from the public treasury, and I give the order to cut off the heads of those who trouble the nation. That is my science. I regard as laudable, however, the desire that others have to learn. It seems to me, though, that in all those books there must be a lot of superfluity. Convene your Academy, which is composed of remarkable and idle men, and command them to compile for you the briefest possible summary of everything essential that the library contains. Thus, you will only take the flower, and you will not have wasted much time.'

"The king found the idea admirable, and immediately passed around his servant's neck the only great sash that he did not yet have. Then he summoned he sages and entrusted his project to them. They did not manifest an excessive enthusiasm, but, after having raised the necessary objections, they set to work.

"Their first surprise was to observe that none of the works comprising the library had ever been read. They were able to assure themselves of that by various signs, particularly the thickness of the dust and the cobwebs. They drew sudden conclusions from that regarding the wisdom of the late king, and plunged as if into a virgin forest into the profundity of the obscure shelves.

"After ten years, the abridgment was concluded. It comprised enough volumes to load a hundred camels. The desolate monarch asked them for a summary of the summary. They came back ten years later. The prince received them coldly. Approaching old age had taken away his illusions. As for the scholars, the majority, having died, had been replaced. Only the leader of the troop remained, who had fortunately been a young man at the beginning. The new précis was still sufficient to load ten camels. The scholars were sent away and you know how, after successive stages and more vanished years, the last of those learned men, exhausted by old age and almost dying, arrived before the king, who was lying on his death-bed. He was just in time, but the summary was contained in a single slim volume.

"'I no longer even have the leisure to read it,' said the king. 'Anyway, what would be the point now? I would, however, have experienced a final joy in knowing, before dying, the science of life.'

"'Sire,' quavered the old man, 'we have been fools. Everything that it is important to know is contained in a single word. We would have found it a long time ago if we had searched outside books.'

"The king sat up, breathlessly, in order to hear the supreme word. The moribund scholar opened his mouth, but only to expire."

"In truth," said Jean Derève, smiling, "we're no further advanced."

Saint-Maur shook his head. "Remember the advice of the priest of fire. A formula only has value by virtue of what it signifies. The supreme word only exists as soon as you understand it. Have good will. Make yourself a child-like soul and lend an ear."

They remained silent.

Suddenly, something strange happened. Jean Derève, a trifle pale, turned to his companion. He had just heard three successive raps struck on the door of the room, separated by an interval of a few seconds. One might have thought that someone outside was knocking in order to be admitted, or to appeal.

"Don't be frightened," said Saint-Maur, "and look. There's no one there, I'm sure of it."

He opened the door widely. Nothing could be seen but the vast and solitary vestibule.

"But perhaps," he continued, "that mysterious appeal is, nevertheless, an appeal. Experiments have been made with wireless telegraphy. From time to time, a mage allows a few principles of occult science to escape. An ignorant but skillful manufacturer immediately makes a material application of it. Exotericism only lives on the alms of esotericism. A fine affair, truly, communication at a distance. There are more conductive threads in nature than humans will ever construct. The dead do not return, but the living can send their image or their idea to other living persons. Do you believe that the will of a distant friend, thinking of you, cannot be manifest by means of some phenomenon or other—a knock at an apartment door, for example? You might tell me that, rigorously, one can suppose the transmission over a distance of a sound, a material phenomenon, but that there is no correlation between a thought and a sound, one being spiritual and the other corporeal. I would ask you then, ingenuously, what matter is, and what spirit is; and you could not give me a response, for none exists. Go to the bottom of all the explanations of philosophers, those who knew that they wanted to say and understood it themselves: spirit, for all of them, is either a less dense matter, or only a word.

"You've followed in the revues the articles of our friend Mathias Corbus. I've often encountered him in your home, but I don't know whether he has authorized you to visit him in his mansard near Notre Dame. Few of his acquaintances have penetrated there. He sits next to his window, from which one can see the towers and buttresses of gray stone. He can amuse himself following the flight of swallows, or divining the thoughts of the grimacing sculptures that stick out their stones head like the laughter of the monument. Or his gray beard inclines over some Hebrew book. He smokes his pipe. There is dust everywhere. The furniture is bizarre. Books are piled up on an apartment organ. There is, however, no crocodile hanging from the ceiling, nor an owl on the wall.

"That romanticism is unimportant. It is only a legitimate amusement devoid of danger. I take much more pleasure in the ideas of that learned man, and I am grateful to him for allowing me to penetrate the elements of his science. We fell, however, into the common error, with regard to communication, of imagining at first that material apparatus was necessary. That is why I had a magic mirror constructed for that correspondence. We consecrated the object in accordance with the rites. The ceremonies of that nature have, at least, the utility of focusing the attention and the will.

"Even with that encumbrance, we obtained excellent results. Two similar mirrors permitted us to put ourselves in relation. We only required a few evenings of patience to project simple geometrical figures at a distance, which the other mirror collected. I shall not say how far we took those experiments, because that is forbidden to me. Be content to know that we progressively diminished, and then suppressed, material aids, as a swimmer exercises at first with apparatus that sustains him, but gradually learns to do without them, and to proceed on his own. You know that at that point there is more liberty with as much security.

"At the present moment, perhaps, by means of that appeal, he desires to take part in our conversation."

There was further silence, and then another three knocks were heard. Saint-Maur collected himself for a few moments, and appeared to listen.

"I'm not mistaken," he exclaimed, "But it isn't to me that the appeal is addressed. Corbus informs me that that he's walking in the Bois nearby and that he's coming to see you. He's heading in this direction. I'll leave you; perhaps I'd be indiscreet. In your place, I'd take advantage of the good weather to go to meet him."

He took his leave. His companion set forth immediately and headed for the wood, a little anxiously.

It was a pleasant April day. The trees had the rich green tint that makes the landscape resemble, at times, a water-color painting. The afternoon atmosphere had a discreet calm. The undergrowth trembled in the distance in a pleasant mist. Many vehicles were seen almost halted by the sidewalks, following with brief pauses rich old men who were trying, the inverse of children, to take their last steps on the arm of an impersonal and clean-shaven valet. The ladies were wearing costumes in which the semi-mourning of the barely-expired winter was shaded by spring. In the tenacious and already gilded dust, bicycles were running, like undulating spiders. Sometimes, the sound of a horn announced an automobile. The vast shadow of a cloud passed over the ground at intervals, setting a fragment of gray ground between two sunlit locations; then the cloud glided over the rounded blue slope toward others extended at the horizon.

What a décor for fantasy, sad or tender, a wood is! Even modern, the forest is still a confidant. One can hang oneself there or make love. Novelists easily suppose encounters on the lawns and conversations on the edge of flat waters where swans navigate slowly. Some have seen hinds move behind the foliage. There are mushrooms at the feet of the large trees, and streams that one passes over on three stones at water level. Here, primitive huts buried in the ground are only revealed by the smoke of dry grass emerging from the chimney. Over there, in the middle of a clearing, a circular shelter of thatch on wooden columns awaits horsemen gone astray in the heart of the forest in the rain. This vague path surely leads to the crossroads where the hunt will be heard sounding the return.

The walker had entered the wood from the direction of Neuilly. More than any others he loved the place in that direction. The route from the gate leaves a melancholy pond to the left, and then traverses a forest of miniature pines. His soul, desirous of calm, welcomed the slightly severe line of those trees, whose trunks rise up like a jet to a majestic height. The healthy odor of fallen twigs, making an elastic layer on the ground, remained him of Mediterranean countries. A vision returned to him with the perfume. If all the senses have a memory, that of perfumes is the most suggestive and causes the most intimate emotions to revive.

Another scene appeared, announced by the forerunning bicycles. One traversed one of the routes reserved for them, where the ground, unified like that of ski-runs, permits smooth riding. The landscape is transformed in accordance with public taste. Stands multiple on the lawns. As caprice or fashion steers toward some horizon, one sees cafes born there like flowers, a few paces from clearings where Puvis de Chavannes found the trees of his sacred wood. A promenade is like a courtesan who changes her dress to please variously.

On leaving the busy thoroughfares, Jean Derève had turned into a pathway that he liked for its dome of foliage. He found himself alone there. Then he perceived, coming from the depths of the pathways, a strolling couple heading toward him. When they came closer he recognized Mathias Corbus, with a certain surprise, in spite of his expectation. A lady was accompanying him. It appeared to him that he had met her before, without him being able to recall where or in what circumstances.

"This is Lucia," said Corbus.

Immediately, the young man had the evening and the temple of fire before his eyes. As the conjectures were connected, Corbus' voice seemed to him to be singularly resonant, like that of the high priest. He imparted his suspicions.

"What a supposition!" Corbus replied. "In any case, one ought not to talk about nocturnal things except at night. We're here to savor the charm of a spring afternoon. Let's imagine that you're going at hazard toward some amorous adventure."

Jean Derève sighed. "You talk about that sentiment as such a simple thing that I envy you. For my part, the joy of amour is like all the others; I search for it, but I haven't found it yet. Or rather, I've only known joys that my anxiety always prevented from being frank."

They took a few paces under the foliage. The young man drew his companions with him. Lucia's face was in the shade of branches cut though by sunlight. Jean Derève could see her more clearly than by night at the temple. She seemed more human and charming. With a hesitation in his first words he continued:

"I once wrote a treatise that I'd give you to read if I still had it, in the manner and style of an Erasmian dialogues. I think it was called *Eutrope, or the Impotence of Loving.*[10] Some men have the strange malady of only being able to attach themselves to that which flees them. No one is more sincere than me when I express my sentiments. However, as soon as they're humanized, I'm astonished to have suffered. I can only cherish those who testify indifference to me. Charm is proportionate to the idea of heartbreak and impossibility. Thus, I can never savor amorous joy, for, when amour comes, joy goes.

"It's also necessary that I lament living, and I only have consciousness of myself by virtue of the memory of a very recent wound. That bitterness is like the salt that conserves and fortifies. I rediscover in my past two very different states of soul, which always succeed one another. Sometimes, I'm haunted by the phantom of a desirable form, which appears impossible to conquer. I suffer; I'd like to annihilate the cause of my torments. I think that only annihilation gives calm, and I appeal with great cries for the forgetfulness of my malaise, but they're false appeals. Sometimes, between two combats, I repose, like a warrior who sees yesterday's enemy disappear, while waiting for other redoubtable arms to surge forth on the horizon with the imminent dawn. But that inaction and that repose become worse than death. And I no longer live in all the time that I don't torture my strange heart in order to amuse it.

---

[10] The reference is presumably to the saint and martyr known in English as Saint Eutropius of Saintes, a hermit who, legend credits with converting Saint Tusetela, the daughter of a Roman governor, who had them both put to death in consequence. There is also a Saint Eutropius of Orange, whose legend seems even less relevant to his evocation in this context.

"Amour and gaiety, for me, are two travelers with hostile faces. When one passes my threshold, the other says adieu. It serves for nothing that at certain hours I've been able to realize the dream so ardently desired. I no longer love amour when it loves me, and I am astonished to have loved. Thus, all I know of it is the apprehension and the anguish. It disappears as soon as it is present. The marble Eros that stands in the middle of my house wounds himself with his own arrows and hides his white wings under an eternal mourning cloak."

"That's doubtless because," Mathias said, "you aren't able to love with the appropriate egotism. I'm prepared to admit with you that the passion that interests you is the sole source of sensuality, but I can't follow you when you affirm, in a self-contradictory fashion that only such a form, at a single moment, is capable of providing it, and that all is lost when one appearance, among all the other possibilities, has disappeared over the horizon. You abandon yourself defenselessly to the pleasure of being enslaved; it's a sad and perverse pleasure. Nothing of what is not ourselves is worth the trouble of bewailing. How one regrets, when other days come, having tortured the heart for a sentiment that was bound to die! Recall your experiences and tell yourself, since you have fortunately proved it, that no emotion is eternal. Don't be saddened by the apprehension that any emotion might not be realized. Don't be disabused if it is realized. Don't dream your life.

"It's necessary to pick the flowers, knowing that they're only flowers, and not to put one's soul into the perfume of one of them, for fear of experiencing too much regret if the perfume vanishes as soon as it is respired. There are women who pass by, some of whom are better to develop your sensibility. You find that amour is sad because you seek more, and also, less, than amour. Above, all, renounce detestable melancholy.

"I believe to be impossible, henceforth, the poets whose genius, true or false, consoled them for not having been loved, or who were loved and tormented themselves in the dread of seeming satisfied. It's a phase that has passed. Humankind was twenty, the age of somber elegies; let us resign ourselves now to our felicity. Joy is within the range of all. It depends on you and not an appearance that hazard has enabled you to encounter. Don't symbolize the voyager who is smitten with a landscape and wants to die for having quit it, nor the one who has no sooner arrived in the landscape that he wants to leave. Different landscapes are at every new horizon. One will be astonished later at the bizarre thought one had of wanting to plant one's tent eternally.

"It's an unfortunate weakness to want to submit one's soul to foreign smiles. Give yourself the amusement of visions that are incessantly new. That way, you will savor amour without ridicule and without treason. Know that the most beautiful faces are only a pretext for the superior play of your divine will. You don't love, just as you don't believe, because you're incapable of making a decision. But if you didn't take any other than that of smiling and being satisfied by that smile, that would already be a great step forward."

"I need help in that," said Jean Derève, "and Saint-Maur spoke to me about you. I don't refuse either belief or action, but I think that the will is susceptible of education and that you might play the role of educator. If artificial means exist, tell me whether I ought to employ them. If, on the contrary, it's sufficient to want in order to be able, I am, in truth, in the best disposition relative to desire. I ask you, and you also: What is it necessary to do to be happy? Do you know the incantations that transmute the soul magically?"

The walkers had arrived at the entrance to the Ranelagh Gardens. It is one of the most intimate shady retreats in Paris. A bandstand forms the center of a lawn strewn with light constructions and children's game. People sometimes play games there in the afternoon, as in provincial towns, and in any case, that fragment of woodland, with its particular physiognomy, evokes certain courtyards or malls of old French cities. Habitués come from neighboring streets in order to smoke pipes or roll hoops, according to age. A meadow alongside the Muette quarter is invaded on holidays by picnickers. Only the tumult of the suburban railway, attenuated by the curtain of trees, serves as a discreet appeal of noisy life arriving from elsewhere.

Mathias Corbus smiled.

"Saint-Maur has spoken to you about poisons that exalt or depress the will. That's a temptation. But we've come a long way from our route. Allow me to take Lucia home. If you want me to come and find you again, we'll continue this important conversation this evening. You can accompany me to other regions. And the night, the mother of obscure thoughts, will favor our discourse."

III. The Green God

Mathias Corbus was at the rendezvous on the edge of the wood. It was the hour when the street-lights were being illuminated and the other life of the city was beginning. After a few minutes, he saw Jean Derève arriving, and both of them, after having consulted one another, descended toward the river by way of sloping streets, through the new constructions that were springing up in those parts.

"If it is necessary to believe historians, the exodus of peoples always takes place from east to west, in the direction of the sun. It seems that humankind, a natural product of the warmth poured out by the star, incessantly marches with it in order to remain under its vivifying influence for as long as possible. Our most ancient memories show us nations, still assembled in families, descending from the high plateaux of Asia when the soil became insufficient for the increased number of human beings. Invasions of barbarians covered Europe successively, and the flow of hordes, like a tide, unfurled over the plains of the continent to come to die definitively, on the beaches of Brittany and Spain, against the other tide of the ocean. But after centuries of apparent repose, the movement recommences, and bold navigators, departing for gold or glory to discover new worlds, are only precursors.

"Like peoples, cities, in their march, follow the course of the sun. Paris develops in that direction, and also that of the river, the two being fortunately parallel on the road of progress. It is natural that one descends more easily than one moves against the current of a watercourse. That is also an influence. The former, however, is the stronger. When they are united their accord gives a perfect result. Everything in the city goes from east to west. Even the lightning obeys that strange commandment. The storms accompany the Seine. It is toward Auteuil and Passy that new houses are constructed. The center of the city, which was once marked by the Place Royale, is moving westwards every day. Life on the boulevards is gradually abandoning one extremity for the other. It is necessary to see in such facts not the manifestation of pure chance but the application of laws as inherent to humankind as its own existence.

"How easy it would be, if one wanted to do it, to multiply those relationships and establish mysterious correspondences that might become clearer by comparison! It is not child's play, but an effort toward unity. It is no use being an observer, if one is content to collect innumerable observations without seeking the connections between them. On the contrary, the person who begins to perceive that everything is similar is marching on the road to truth. At every step his thought penetrates one of the secrets of nature. It glimpses the great secret, the simplicity and the harmony.

"The puerilities of the ancients sometimes have the same profound meaning as the modern visions. Empedocles compares the Earth to a vast animal of which forests are the hair and the divine sea the sweat. Evidently, such comparisons sin in that they take as reality one of the objects of comparison and want the other to be identified with it, instead of supposing that the two are different projections of the same law. But it is also necessary to admit, in those phrases, more than wordplay. We make Paris the heart of the world without expressing anything by the vocable other than a striking analogy. How do we know that there isn't a more rigorous similarity?

"One can, for instance, look at the maps of Paris found in the carriages of the circular railway as little images rotating around their object. The red line of the limit gives the strange form of a heart, with a regular depression at the corresponding point, turned, moreover toward the west, as if drawn by the sun. A puerile assimilator might pursue the comparison, which does not go very far. The mountains and the woods, and the river, the great artery, lent themselves to ingenious reasoning. The idea, following its route, falls into paradox, but is it not sufficient for astonishment that one can find such pretext for the game, which seems plausible.

"Nothing is known. The world is infinite, but the same forms ought to appear at all the levels of infinity. We must be for some what others are for us. The animalcules that live on the surface of our body doubtless, surely, have glorious civilizations, and inexpiable wars for the possession of the area between two pores of our skin. Reflections of that nature enable scorn for the infantile brain of a Napoléon. Earths surged forth from the sun like globes of fire cool slowly, and the crystallizations produced at their surface are the dwellings, temples and palaces of human beings, with their silky and emotional life. The same phenomena appear on the sparks sprung from our hearth during the brief moment, relative to their magnitude, before they become grains of cold ash, like the dead moon in the sky.

"We only know the beings that are on the scale of our eyes. Animalcules do not suspect the personal reality of our body. Nor can we say anything about the immense body on the surface of which we agitate childishly. All hypotheses remain plausible and are lost, one after another, in the void of our thought. But it would be strange if our body alone were endowed with consciousness and other assemblages of material elements were all deprived of it, for the entertainment of our pride."

Jean Derève and Mathias Corbus had passed Les Invalides, saluting in passing the bridge of arches of alliance launched in honor of barbaric borrowers of the north and had taken the Boulevard Saint-Germain at the Pont de la Concorde. Paris was animated in the special atmosphere of the evening. They approached the warm streets where youth exasperates its desire to live and numb itself in the light, far into the night. They passed groups of students and artists, accompanied by young women, some of whom were pretty.

"The pretty girls launched into voluptuous circulation every day head for this quarter in small numbers, because it forms a city within the city, less Parisian than provincial, with its floating population and its sellers of the illusions with which twenty-year-old appetites are content. The future advocates or physicians, a little sad to have seen the old brasseries disappear, play at house and manille with women who are often also from the provinces, and who populate that Babel in which the unfortunate confusion of languages reigns. Observers who reappear, by virtue of a slightly perverse taste, in the milieux through which they once passed, note one evening by chance the face of a charming young woman whom they will not find the next day, rapidly abducted. Those who remain, in growing old, take on a redoubtable aspect.

"More interesting forms are encountered in painters' studios. But again, the good models present irreproachable parts of the body more often than faces. It is better, then to contemplate a marble, for the body only has its flower of expression in the smile and the gaze. All beautiful bodies are similar. It is the eyes that change them, and the lips that allow the various souls within them to become transparent. It is difficult for a man to die of regret for a beautiful form if he has not initially been seduced by the special charm of the face, and by the play of physiognomy that enables a woman to be herself and not a random other. In spite of the philosophy of Plato, what attaches us to the beloved is not beauty, but *her* beauty. That is so true that everyone searches eternally for the same features. The man who has been abandoned turns round when he perceives on passing, even ugly, someone who reminds him of the lost gesture. It is possible to remain indifferent to the most authentic grace that is not that of yesteryear.

"And how few heads really have an expression! One ought not, it is true, reason from merchants of pleasure. It is too easy, by taking illusory examples, to demonstrate that amour is an illusion. Glimpsed in the evening, under artificial light, some of them, at least, seem to have a personality. The hair and the hat, the different usage of make-up or speech separates one from another, and can, for a few minutes, stimulate special curiosities in the human beast. But with what amazement one observes, on awakening after the good or bad night, that, taking advantage of the obscurity, a demon expert in facile jokes has come to place on the shoulders of the occasional lady, in exchange for yesterday's face, the same colorless and banal head. They are all the same when morning comes. It is an observation made by young men whom the rigor of fate condemns, as well as their sentimental idleness, to similar amours. But they perceive subsequently that those women, fortunately, are not all women."

The two strollers had sat down, fatigued by a true voyage, on the terrace of a noisy café. The interior light spread out violently over the sidewalk. Young women were circulating between the tables. Fragments of witty conversation could be heard from neighboring groups.

Mathias Corbus and Jean Derève leaned back, the soul abandoned like the body in the nonchalance of a public bath. They summoned a waiter, who brought them coffee and beer.

"You mentioned Saint-Maur," said Mathias, "and you expect me to reveal to you, more explicitly than him, what secret of dreams is included in the usage of poisons. You desire that they transport you to the ideal realm where existence is happy and the game of personality becomes facile. I disapprove of those procedures. Too numerous are those who demand from accursed substances an embellishment of life, however illusory. The attempt can be profitable, however, if it is not excessively prolonged.

"Some people are idle or dare not develop their power. One day, by chance, under a new influence, they sense that they are living differently. It is not, believe me, merely to savor a dubious pleasure, of which one is never sure, that one should make such attempts. It happens that an unusual shock suddenly shows a person his soul. Morphine and opium enable an unknown sensibility to surge forth from the depths. What a temptation for the man to whom those new emotions are revealed! What a desire to rise, if not without danger, at least without effort, above surly life! 'It's necessary to be intoxicated,' as Baudelaire says, "by wine, opium or poetry.' But the man who is intoxicated ceases to be himself, in the good as well as the bad sense.

"The dream is evidently to conciliate enthusiasm and clarity, to retain the direction of one's being and at the same time to abandon oneself to charming influences. A very difficult accord, I fear. Perhaps only those are right who do not care about obtaining from poisons an increase of their energy but who only seek enchantment and forgetfulness. Too frequently, life is a bad dream; and one ought to be indulgent to the invalids who demand the liberating opium loudly. Existence easily becomes sinister when one has some sensibility.

"The man who does not arouse the ardor of a profound passion drags himself along lamentably. Fortunate are martyrs and saints! Fortunate is the cenobite who prays in the cold silence of the cell and sobs toward God! All those of us who agitate in a puerile manner do not even succeed in the miserable enterprise of amusing ourselves. For my part, I am interested in certain things, and I spend my days appropriately. I regard myself as satisfied, because I am not ambitious; and I have not found unhelpful, in order to give myself at intervals a different vision, and seize various aspects, the usage of certain drugs, of which my curiosity has, in any case, never made me a slave. But it would be infantile to allow oneself to be mastered and to live under an influence. I have sampled all intoxications, but I have known, by contrast, at other times, the charm of asceticism. And I have become capable—this alone is important—of suggesting to myself the most various states of soul, simply by the exercise of my will. I have told you that additives are only profitable in order to learn to do without them.

"They are numerous, and their choice varies in accordance with countries and people. Women take morphine, and so do physicians, on occasion. It is the unfortunate remedy for insupportable pain. But the danger is that one contracts therefrom a mortal malady whose course is interrupted. I am also repelled by the surgical procedure. I believe that opium smoking, with its immobile dreams, is better suited to idle socialites. It also possesses navigators from Oriental lands, who have retained after their return the habits acquired out there. But the material difficulties are an obstacle to the diffusion. Furthermore, the initiation is rather slow. That last inconvenience is not unique to opium. It has saved many hesitant individuals.

"The people have wine and alcohol, of which it is better not to speak.

"You know that in Ireland, ether is propagating rapidly, completing the annihilation, by new means, of the vague inhabitants of that country.[11] The drug has primarily physical effects. It gives an extraordinary lightness of body and mind. Perhaps you have occasionally eaten strawberries dipped in ether. But the insupportable and persistent odor hardly permits a correct man to give himself to that vice; everyone perceives his mania. I have a horror of manifestations and involuntary confessions. In any case, it seems to me that there can be no question of drinking ether. The taste, even dissimulated by mixtures, is disagreeably intense. I believe that one obtains sufficient impressions by sniffing a flask. The brain is rapidly

---

[11] Ether-drinking became something of a craze in Ireland in the 1880s before it was curtailed by law in 1891, when ether was classified as a poison and strict controls introduced on its sale and distribution. Modern sources suggest that it was popularized by a physician named Kelly, who marketed it as a medicament, and was widely taken up in a backlash against the Temperance Movement, allowing people who had "made the Pledge" to get drunk without having to consume alcohol.

affected and one arrives without difficulty at the state of fortunate semi-consciousness in with everything around one is blurred, in which sounds and visions are metamorphosed and attenuated, although our senses, instead of losing their acuity, acquire an astonishing and seemingly fragile sensibility.

"Although ether is in the first rank among the accursed beverages, it is improbable that opium, of which I have spoken, can be known in its real effects by the usage of laudanum. The complicated apparatus of smokers would be inexplicable if a few drops of liquid had the same virtue. That is undoubtedly not the case. It is necessary to smoke the resin, in the Oriental fashion. Our mores do not permit that easily. And I conclude therefrom, for everything has a cause, that the usage of the poison necessitates certain habits that we do not have. It is suited to the temperaments of hot countries, where the soul willingly follows the slope of torpor. The liquid extract scarcely provokes anything but visual impressions, or, rather, an amusing deformation of vision. All stupefiants, in any case, by means of the dilatation of the pupils, act in that regard to a greater or lesser extent.

"I believe, moreover, that a person who uses one or other of those substances habitually, will not experience very different effects if he tries a new one in passing. Sensitivity exasperated in a certain direction retains a tendency to the same awakenings. A hashish-eater taking opium or ether one day, by virtue of necessity or curiosity, will have that day, as usual, a hashish intoxication.

"I don't know whether that observation has been noted before. I don't believe so.

"One can also observe that it is dangerous to mix. That increases immeasurably the unfortunate impression that results from the absorption of various wines. The most deplorable of my memories is of that nature. I had sampled Indian hemp with a morphinomane that I did not know as such. The modifications of his self, of course, from the picturesque viewpoint, were those of morphine, but the nervous disturbance was multiplied tenfold. He had a frightful crisis. I believed seriously that he was going to die. He swore to me that he would never have the fantasy of renewing that experiment. It was sufficient.

"You have present in mind the accounts of Baudelaire and Théophile Gautier. They are excellent studies of the cult of the green god. There are curious pages in the work of Alexandre Dumas père that are amusing. I suspect him of having employed hashish to amplify some of his descriptions, for example, the grotto of Monte Cristo. I shall talk to you shortly about the imaginative influence that renders the substance dear and redoubtable to litterateurs and musicians. But the notes that they have left, or the works that they wrote with that obscure unavowed collaboration, are, from all points of view, documents more precious, although not technical, than the brochures of physicians on this subject. That is because it is absolutely necessary in order to describe such effects, to have experienced them oneself. There does not exist in any language a true poem of amour having as its author a man who had not loved.

"Physicians, practical men, have only been able to note and utilize one bizarre property of the poison, the prodigious overstimulation of the sensation of hunger. It is very discomfiting to go to dinner, especially the first time, after taking hashish, with people who are not habituated to eating it. With a moderate dose one can, for instance, render appetite to consumptives. Another excellent influence might also be produced in the latter case, by which I mean a general excitation of vital activity. But how many physicians, men of science, are interested in what might be called, in science, experimentation? They prefer to employ their time searching for hypothetical microbes or serums that it is necessary to hasten to take, while they cure by fashionability and suggestion.

"There is no lack of benevolent subjects for the experiment. The vice is very contagious. One finds the green poison in a great many pharmacies, of course, but in the same way that one does not procure remarkable wines from the usual merchants, it is not always the perfect drug. The inferior product, however, well prepared and in good condition, produces sufficient effects. Certain inhabitants of the city, of bourgeois and calm appearance, go in search at regular intervals if their provision of dreams. In their souls, without a doubt, the visions of Hoffmann and Poe pass. There are aulic councilors haunted by the green demon.

An extract in pill form can also be replaced by a liquid extract. The formula was given to me, in fact, by a pharmacist who had doubtless succumbed in serving the passion of others. He lives in the vicinity of the Arc de Triomphe. He gave me a bottle that I left to another of my friends, not daring to make use of it myself. The pharmacist was the most colorless man I ever saw. Under the smiling and indulgent gazes of his pupils, he poured a few drops from the green bottle over a sugar lump, which he absorbed with an expression of joyful ecstasy. Then he went through the streets looking for popular celebrations, searching for material to his dream, entirely happy, giving the impression of being slightly mad.

"People sometime also use flower-heads of the plant, which are smoked. There is an old herborist's shop in a narrow street near the Seine, at the back of a courtyard. But it is necessary to be skillful to distinguish, by smoking the leaves of French and Indian hemp. That usage is, moreover, not always excellent. One experiences impressions similar to those given by smoking tea. I do not know what effects an extract of tea put into pills has.

"But let us note that it is necessary not to think—and one ought to add, by any formula of persuasion—of returning to the normal taste of tobacco a pipe that has know, even if only once, the charm of Indian hemp. It will retain for the rest of its life an abominable bitterness. One must resolve no longer to fill it with other leaves than the accursed ones. You can see there, without effort, a symbol of passions that poison one's soul forever. Let us note that in order to please the old moralist who slumbers, with his spectacles and his head on his breast, in the depths of the soul of each of us."

During Mathias' discourse, the animation of the street had died down. The café became deserted. A few belated couples were seen on the terrace exchanging inferior amorous words. The two conversationalists got up. Two o'clock had just chimed. They walked along the boulevards. That is when the glimpsed banks of the Seine and the Cathedral recall Victor Hugo.

"Are you sleepy?" said Jean Derève.

"A sage is never somnolent. That axiom is found in book six of the Bhagavata, paragraph thirty. It won't rain tonight. We have eternity to sleep."

Jean Derève smiled. "May the Eternal put on our lips, before sealing the sepulcher, a strong dose of opium or hashish!"

"No, dreams are only produced in moderate sleep, and death is probably a profound sleep. It's true that one cannot foresee the effects exactly in accordance with the measure of the poison. Some are astonished and do not experience any result. The influence depends greatly on the present disposition. It's also necessary to distinguish between the different forms: jam, extract or leaves. Gautier speaks about the jam, a mixture with a perfumed vehicle. It has a slightly sickening taste. In that form, hashish only has a very attenuated influence, slothful, so to speak. It is, I think in those conditions that the Orientals use it. But everything is transformed by temperament. The native of Indo-China smokes an opium pipe lying on a mat, which is sufficient to give birth to his somewhat animalistic dream. Thomas De Quincey, the man of the North, the Englishman with robust nerves—because he was English, albeit slightly mad, being a poet—felt deprived when he did not have a large carafe of laudanum on his work-table.

"The observations that I have been able to make all bear upon people using pills. That is the most convenient form. One can easily carry with one the pretext of the dream; and it's truly an amusing problem to pose that so many visions can be enclosed in a globule of green paste. They really are, since, once the globule is absorbed, they go to deploy in our brain, displaying to our inner vision a crazy, charming, colorful pantomime. The effect is rapid or slow, and is not produced, in any case, in everyone. For some, who are refractory in one way or another, there is only a bizarre shock, a brief and painful disturbance of the brain. Or, again, the impression lasts, but is purely physical and utterly unbearable. There are nervous tremors, convulsions of the eyes and inarticulate moans, indicating a profound suffering. One stops at a first experiment, with the sentiment of having had a narrow escape, like tobacco smokers to whom the first cigarette gives vertigo. Those accidents are rare, and for habitués they are produced no more frequently than the others for a habitual tobacco smoker. It requires very unfavorable circumstances, an already existent malaise, or an exaggerated dose. With elementary precautions, they are never produced.

"Among all sorts of experiments there are bad cases. Only reasoning from them is taking rare exceptions for the rule. Does the opinion of an inexperienced smoker make the law for tobacco? Does a person whose stomach only accepts milk cut with mineral water have the right to affirm doctorally that drunkenness does not exist and that Bacchic poets are liars? And that the drunkenness of wine, however, must be crude, and devoid of charm besides?

"That is the error into which I saw a talented young novelist, known for well-written, modern works of fortunate development, fall one day. He witnessed a séance at which I was present, which was deplorable. Two neophytes were ill. One suffered a malady of the stomach with sharp crises, accompanied by vertigo. The other was a very advanced morphinomane. The novelist, whose unique and only observation it was, never wanted to admit that it was not inclusive. He wrote thereafter a chapter of a book in a definitive tone. It would have been pointless to sustain to him that he would only have the right to give a serious opinion after other observations made on normal individuals. Bacon's laws, for him, assuredly, were a dead letter. He did not suspect that, for science, the isolated fact does not exist. I conceived vehement doubts after that about the verity of his books and the documentary value of his descriptions.

"For normal temperaments, in a period that lasts from a few minutes to a few hours and ends up being limited similarly in the same person, the effect arrives suddenly. It is a seizure of the sensibility as abrupt as it is absolute, a kind of reasoned vertigo, for wanting it, one can remain master of oneself and assist one's folly. The patient is well aware that he is dreaming, but like a traveler sitting in an enchanter's carriage, who can direct it on condition of not getting out of it. You did not have to make a great effort to divine that, a little while ago, as well as relating notes made on others I was talking about myself. There is no impression newer and more moving than that of having the soul gripped by that poison.

"The first day that I used it was one of the days of my life. My incredulity underwent the strangest of revelations. I had been walking for a few hours with the old poet Lélian,[12] who died five or six years later. It was time to go back. My furtive intoxication went back an hour or two, and I was waiting, with a slight anguish, to be alone with my impressions. There was no other symptom apart from that expectation.

"That evening, the Bohemian genius had received 'a few golds,' as he put it, and I accompanied him toward the Montagne Sainte-Geneviève, where he lived, lavishing the most virtuous advice on him as we went. He listened to me, shaking his head like a bald bear with the greatest gravity. He recognized the wisdom of what I was saying. The moment had come to astonish public opinion by the sober rigor of his life. What a pity to spend nights drinking in order to ruin oneself. He was

---

[12] In Paul Verlaine's classic study of *Les Poètes maudits* (1884), the author includes himself under the anagrammatical pseudonym "pauvre Lélian."

going to return immediately to his room on the fourth floor of a modest house.

"We walked on. With his cloak, his vast hat and his staff, he resembled a grim shepherd. Our silhouettes became rather vague under the moonlight in that old quarter. I remember that in one narrow street that rose up in pointed cobblestones between two rows of Medieval houses, I arrived at accents whose eloquence would have made the most hardened sinner dissolve in tears. Without taking account of it, I was under the influence that had arrived.

"We separated on the poet's threshold, after great protestations. He closed the door with a gesture that I divined, in the vestibule, to be Roman. And I drew away, in the moonlight, which outlined in black the gables of the facades on the descending route, refraining from turning round, divining that he was watching, from behind the furtively-reopened door, for me to turn the first corner in order to go impenitently to his culpable pleasures. With our fine assurance, in that solitary and nocturnal décor, like two people who are not dupes but are putting on a very good semblance, we had played a charming scene from an Italian comedy.

"I would not have employed that expression if the property of the poison were not precisely to solemnize all encounters and give them a theatrical appearance. A majestic fever takes possession of you. The slightest incidents take on an infinite value. Has it not happened to me, lying in an armchair, to spend long minutes contemplating a ceiling rose, finding an inexpressible grandeur in the vision of those ordinary but regular designs? Music, beautiful verses heard, and the landscape, all acquire a profound charm. Life becomes amusing and easy. It is as if the hand of a mage has passed a fresh new color over everything. A pretext is not even necessary. Each wave of intoxication that rises to the brain evaporates in evocative clouds. And there is at the same time, as in dreams, the unexpectedness of images, the repose, for a few hours, of effort, and a playful activity, in a divine torpor. Imagine that folly is striking your head, slowly and repeatedly, with a golden hammer.

"It is the same mental disposition as in a dream, with, it is true, the inconvenience of the artifice employed. If one could create such a state of soul naturally, one would be similar to the gods. I've often thought what joy that ability would give us. The mysterious law of dreams has not been studied sufficiently. But remember the most beautiful ones you have had. No real voluptuousness approaches it. Suppose now that, without losing the charming insouciance, you were capable of directing your impressions, and that, above all, you were not at the brutal mercy of awakening. For men endowed with that admirable genius, it would then only be a matter of overturning the usual order of existence. One would spend upright the few hours necessary to physical life; but once the tasks were accomplished, everyone would plunge back into the evocative night, like a fatigued worker who sees every evening the door of an unknown palace opening, of which he is the king.

"The direction of dreams!

"If it is true that in slumber, we only rediscover, in a bizarre and new order, the impressions of the previous day, we could make from those known elements an unusual masterpiece, as painters and sculptors have borrowed the head or the wings of some vulgar beast in order to create a chimera that does not exist. And how do we know that our eyes are not give to us to see and our ears to hear the scattered colors or sounds with which we compose, when night falls, the painting or opera of genius? The persistence of the soul and its slight consciousness, when it is liberated from exterior things is perhaps the one proof of our immortality. It allows us to comprehend that we are still alive, that we are respiring with an ardent and sure breath, even and especially when we have folded over our thought the darkness that protects us, as a child sleeps in a bedroom with closed windows, which the noises of the street cannot reach, and which a discreet lamp populates with dreams. But it is evidently necessary only to speak of people with sufficient mastery of their obscure soul to be able to read the pages of the book that the crowd cannot open. For the majority, sleep is a brief but absolute death; and if they have dreams, they are anxious about that abnormal phenomenon. Thus, animals, except for a few superior ones, do not dream.

"That freedom from matter, that communion in sleep with a divine soul, was the origin of belief in prophetic divinations. The soul of the Earth was revealed to sleepers in the lair of Trophonius. The state of dreaming is superior to that of wakefulness. It is better to see with closed eyes, to hear without ears. It is a superb joy to observe that the organs can disappear without the rest of us being annihilated.

"But of all that mystery I can only retain one sole verity, the absence of effort, the spontaneity, the rapidity of thought, the supple unfurling of visions. It is in that respect that the intoxication of which we speak can be compared with usual dreams. The voluptuousness that it provides is also a liberation. Certain essential stages can be noted, however, in the duration of that joy, for it is easier to observe and abstract the laws of the waking dream than the other. The first impression is a frank and intense gaiety. One the evening that I told you about, after quitting the poet, in the exquisite décor, I had fits of silent laughter, as after an amusing act well played. And it was by that bizarre and excessive hilarity that I recognized being henceforth under the impression.

"Although the manifestations vary with diverse temperaments, few people escape that absurd nervous laughter. A man exuberant in the normal state then becomes redoubtable. He will make a series of puns to supply all the bearers of almanacs for ten years, even in the most obscure provinces, with old French gaiety. In many people, moreover, that period is the entire crisis. It is also necessary that they be capable of some awakening. Stupid souls feel nothing. Malevolent souls, on the other hand, even in that first phase, are frightfully revealed. I have had in hashish, without provoking them, confidences painful by virtue of the sudden light that they cast on the dirtiness of certain consciences that I knew vaguely. The intoxication is, at any rate, favorable to frankness. But intellectual intoxication ought to be redoubted by all those whose soul is vile. Moral ugliness is reflected as if in a magnifying mirror. Let such people remain in silence and in their obscurity. I see there a magic realm the door of which is eternally closed to them. They will not know the charming and veritable effect of hashish.

"It would be puerile to remark that people denuded of intelligence are even more denuded of it, although they astonish themselves at that moment; or they say vulgar things. On the contrary, nothing is as amusing as conversation with people of agreeable commerce. Everything favors the blossoming of a particular humor. The beginning is a slightly feverish expectation, mingled with incredulity. One is unaware of the effects. One does not know from which direction the seductive demon will come, and one looks furtively at the doors, and the mirrors that are the doors of the occult. Everyone is slightly arrogant.

"The tendency exists to make fun of the credulous who anticipate unusual things. One makes jokes at their expense and one laughs—except that the laughter gradually takes on a special quality and rings with a new timbre. The person who does not suspect it suddenly finds that he is under an unusual influence, with the vehement and grateful desire to cry: '*Ecce deus!*' He is not alone; his fit is contagious. The craziest visions emanate from the most futile incident. A charming good grace lends itself obligingly; any word pronounced takes on unexpected significance. It is the bizarre impression noted by Thomas De Quincey, for whom, in opium, the mere words 'Roman consul' evoked Roman armies, triumphs and all the grandiose apparatus of legends and paintings.

"The soul is at the mercy of its dreams and the imagination. External vision is subject in that regard to bizarre modifications. One looks at one of one's neighbors; one is astonished to see his face and to find it irresistibly comical. One starts to preach to him, with a gravity agitated by spasms, the necessity of changing his face as soon as possible. I have heard some hashishins make speeches with an incoherence and an abundant fantasy that would have made the fortune of a fairground barker, but it is like a light froth that gradually fades away and vanishes. The conversation is all verbal acrobatics. The wordplay is entangled and enchained with an unexpected logic that seems dazzling. Exuberant joy, a veritable physical sensuality, is betrayed by profound respirations and colored faces. The cheeks are dolorous and the eyes haggard.

"That period is variable in duration: an hour or two, sometimes a whole evening or an entire night. The fatigue that flows is proportionate. Observe, in any case, that it is difficult to render an accurate account of the duration. In hashish, as in opium, space and time are deformed. For philosophers, space and time, simple *a priori* forms of sensibility, do not exist in themselves. They are convenient forms for disposing our impressions, which contract or extend to the desired dimensions. An insect that lives for a day has an existence as long as that of a carp or a crow. Everything is relative. We cannot count the minutes except by means of the successive thoughts that we have had. A dreamless night appears to us as rapid as a lightning flash. We know, on the other hand, that some nocturnal vision, which we believed to last or hours, unfurled in a second. Joyful sentiments, and above all painful ones, permit us to measure our life. They are the white or black milestones that reveal the road traveled; and the more urgent those sentiments are, the fuller and more real the moment seems to us.

"But how much more rapid our march is between the white markers than the black ones! Eternities go by in hours of waiting behind the curtain of the window, while listening for the advent of the noise of a distant carriage, which increases, which is going to stop, and with always goes past our house. Those hours do not have the same duration as those that fly by at the feet of a beloved woman, saying puerile things to her.

"Is not the flow of time always equal, and the fall of the sand in the hourglass no more hasty or retarded? In hashish, sudden visions succeed one another with such rapidity that we believe that we live years of joy in a minute. For how long are you plunged in that ocean with golden and voluptuous waves? How many waves have brushed you, lulled you, and carried you away tumultuously? You look at the clock. Its hands do not seem to have moved. One can lead one's existence at the pace one wishes. The man who has a passion for living beauty or for art has lived more in one day than the bodies with monotonous gesture that we see passing indistinctly in the street have in their entire terrestrial presence.

"And like time, space, which is correlated with it, since it is measured by time, acquires a rare elasticity on those occasions. I have retained the memory of evenings when, after a distant séance, I was returning home on foot. What fatigue! The route stretched desperately. I thought about Petit Poucet in the forest, who saw a red window shining through the distant trees, and who went toward the light without ever being able to get closer to it. Add that, in order to climb the steps of my staircase, it would have been advantageous to me to have borrowed his boots, each step being, in my imagination, at least a meter high. It also required, in order in move, even with that difficulty, a certain impetus.

"In the first experiments, it often happens in certain subjects that all the functions of relation are suspended. Later, one gets used to it, one can come and go, but still with unusual impressions that give one a slightly astonishing gait. With experience, one corrects them, knowing their falsity. They gradually disappear as one achieves more self-mastery. There is, in any case, a surprise in any initiation, from all viewpoints, which subsequently loses its novelty."

The two companions had run aground in a restaurant near Les Halles, and while charting, gazed through the cigarette smoke at the noctambulatory figures scattered in the air around them. There were young women in quest of amour who were contenting themselves with a supper. Men in worn garments were drinking with them. Some ordered complicated drinks with a weary expression. At the back of the room three musicians around a piano remained silent for a moment; then their hands took the violins with a sudden decision. The notes of a waltz departed furiously, then languished, and shreds of the melody were heard through the appeals of drunkenness or disputes. Sometimes, two women enlaced one another and danced to the music, and then returned to their places. The ceremony continued with the passage of a saucer in a solicitous hand though the scantly charms audience, in which coins clinked. There was a repose, and the same ritual was celebrated with the same details.

The timid daylight appeared, as if through a fog. The large windows became pale with a diffuse light. Shadows could be seen passing by on the sidewalk.

"The second period," Mathias Corbus continued, "is announced by a calming in the laughter and the games. The conversation is more discreet. Profound thoughts, or those thought to be, supplant the puerile fantasies. It is the moment when people amuse themselves constructing philosophical systems and cosmogonies. Everything seems easy. The mind plays with ideas, or ideas play with the mind. Nothing troubles the serenity. It is an assembly of gods around the nectar and the ambrosia, letting fall in a slow and rich voice words imprinted with solemnity. And each member of the audience, in fact, believes himself to be a god. One experiences a disdainful pity for vain usual cares.

"That ecstasy, in some people, takes on a contemplative form. They follow an interior image, the colors and lines of which have no equivalent in real life, or, rather, take the present sensation—sound, décor or perfume—as a theme. I have memories. One evening was spent at a good classical concert, in which I heard a triumphal march, so majestic and so moving that my heart was oppressed and, in order not to cry out with delight or faint with joy, I was obliged to go outside to respire the appeasing night air. Another time, in a drawing room whose furniture was pure Louis XV—that is the style of hashish—I had a conversation with a woman whose garments, appearance and smile were miraculously harmonious. No more was necessary. They were impressions of absolute art.

"But equally, when one is fortunate enough to encounter intimate friends, one abandons oneself to the discussion of fine subjects. One thinks that no one has ever had such imagination, richer verbal treasures, such ease in navigating among arguments and images. Things said appear to be admirable, even the charm disappears. It sometimes happens, as in dreams, that one follows brilliant thoughts, delighted by having conceived them, and one sees them gradually fade way and lose their luster as one awakens, to be reduced, in the broad daylight of consciousness to some absurd or childishly grotesque phrase. That is rare. The interest often remains, in an indecent or vulgar fashion. It is the tendency of hashish to give substance to the strangest conceptions.

"I was so gripped, that day, by the material effect of the poison, that I did not have the strength to open a drawer for sheets of paper, and I noted the pantomime on the envelopes of letters that happened to be under my hand. When I reread them, there were twenty written leaves, with tedious and infantile repetitions, fragments of verse, refrains, an entire mass that I had to eliminate in order to reduce the work to five or six pages, crazy but amusing. You will find the fragment in a volume of poems in prose that I published, almost all the pages of which were written under the same inspiration.

"In the beginning, one is still too troubled to make a reasoned usage, but after some time the manifestations differ. The classic crisis no longer existing, one steers the excitation in the desired direction. If one eventually gets the habit—I don't advise you to acquire it—and you want to furnish a considerable effort at a certain moment, absorb a pill in the evening. Renew the dose two or three hours later if the effect is insufficient. Have a light meal about half an hour later and set to work. You will be fortunate to retain for three or four hours a light tendency, a facility of elaboration, an ease in thought and phrase that you have never known. Everything that you do will be extraordinarily interesting for you. If it is a work of science, the most arid research will have flavor. If it is a matter of poetry, new images, a source of joy, will crowd before your eyes. It is important, as I have indicated, to reread what you have written later. You will find such incoherencies in what had enthused you that they will make you smile. But passages will remain that you would not have composed without metaphors and visions whose color survives.

"You might raise the objection of the dangers. To take the written page and compose—for what I have said also applies to music—under an influence is to risk impotence in the normal state. That rule is not absolute, for the impetus acquired persists even beyond the moment. And then, the habitués will reply that it does not matter, if they find better inspirations. There remains the physical peril and the disturbance of the heart or brain to dread. But that is the ransom.

"Do not listen to the donkeys who do not want any intoxication, even of genius. They reproach Musset for his intemperance, without wondering whether it was not the exaggeration and the fatal consequence of a disposition useful to his work. Posterity will not know that the poet as a drinker. He had the penalty of his passion, he will have the merit. Strictly speaking, he was a martyr, if you wish. And if one is conscious that the poison is developing within us, perhaps, an unknown virtue, which has not been revealed, what true artist would not accept to see his life abridged, if he had the assurance, by means of that offering, that he would create the beautiful form and realize his ideal?

"The objection would be the same, and more forceful, for disinterested employment. The person who only seeks pleasure will experience the baleful effects of hashish more than another, since he abandons himself to his impressions instead of directing them. It is impossible that a good fortune of that nature should not be expiated. Prudence can attenuate the bad consequences, but it is rare that one will not experience them, one day or another, by virtue of an exaggerated dose or an unfavorable disposition, I knew one unfortunate who suffered heart palpitations for several weeks after his first experiment, like those soldiers of amour who are mortally wounded in the first battle. Some people are unlucky.

"I came out of a house one evening in order to return home in a state of confusion that did not leave me the strength to hail a cab to transport me. As each vehicle went past I represented to myself in advance the intense effort that I would have to make in order to summon the coachman, open the door and give my address, all with sufficient calm that the man would not think me insane. It was necessary not to think of it. All that I could do was walk like a somnambulist straight ahead, on a route that unfurled like a veritable Calvary. Oh, the

torture of sensing one's thoughts vagabonding and fleeing! There is no worse torture for a self-controlled man
who does not want to abandon himself.

"As I marched, it appeared to me that, from one minute to the next, my heart was going to stop beating, for
physical pain was mingled with mental apprehension, or
that I was about to be overwhelmed by a misfortune that
as following me. I was like those unfortunates who say
to themselves: 'One more effort, one more step. If I get
as far as that, I'm saved...' And the anguish was re-
newed, with alternatives of better and worse, for there is
a rhythm in hashish, and terror comes in successive
waves after moments of calm. I asked myself, without
daring to reply, at what blessed station my torture would
come to an end.

"But often, having returned home, I did not find repose. I have spent frightful nights imploring slumber,
sensing my brain congested and terrified by my heart.
Sometimes, it beat as if to burst. Sometimes, with cold
sweats, I lost it beneath my hand. My breast was as motionless as that of a corpse. And as it is necessary that
the bizarre, even in the tragic, never loses its preroga-
tives, I was desolated by the idea that it would be impossible for me, in spite of the most laudable contortions, to
put an ear to my breast in order to ausculate myself.

"One can, however, attenuate those tortures, which
come from a sort of vertigo of the stomach. It is necessary to take astringents. I have seen people experience
good effects by eating a lemon. Cold water is also a
good remedy. But the best remedy is to reassure oneself
by thought that the malaise is, fundamentally, not dangerous and will soon pass. The most radical treatment
would doubtless be never to take hashish again.

"What is one to do? It is futile to want strange sensations if one is not disposed to expiate them. Every man who is preoccupied with living an intense life commits, if one still supposes that kind of reasoning, a sin that must be punished. What joy is not redeemed by a pain? The sovereign law of equilibrium is never found in default. Who can tell whether there is not a mysterious appeal in dread itself? Danger is seductive because it is redoubtable. It would truly be too good if one could play with weapons and philters without risking death. Then again, one ought to congratulate oneself on proofs from which fear dissuades vulgar souls. But the tortures of hashish, like those of opium, are very little for the man who has had the joys.

"I am talking about profound joys. Among all those who seek them, only a small number have known them. As well as moderation, certain safeguards need to be in place. But it is possible, at times, to enter the forbidden country. One of my finest memories is that of an excursion by carriage, along deserted streets—for all my landscapes are of cities—with forgotten women, one evening in May. They were singing softly, and their voices, very banal, suddenly became divine. We were passing over a bridge. I had the sudden, absolute vision of snowflakes falling around me. The sadness of that unreal snow in the warm night, the music of the songs, and the silent décor of the houses, all carried me far away. I have never had a moment more perfect in my life. One might have thought that we were going, murmuring, beneath falls of white wings, to the burial of a Pierrot who had died of amour, in order to put Basque tambourines and fans in wreaths on the funeral cart.

"Such hallucinations are rare. There are others that I cannot recount. The story would only have meaning for initiates. One must also refrain from the poison in painful hours, for it amplifies all the scenes and different states of the soul. But go, after having absorbed it, to a concert or to contemplate a painting. Go for a walk in a well ordered park or an unexpected forest. Have light around you, especially candlelight, smiles, beautiful gestures bright and silky garments. Hashish is a lover of luxury, as well as a diabolical sower of fear. Infernal forms, if you are not careful, will haunt your nights. You will believe that you are immured for eternity in a sepulcher, with phosphorescences grimacing in the blackness around you.

"But more frequently you will find yourself in a series of red rooms with hangings and candelabras. You have arrived for a celebration and you know that soon, a strange ceremony will take place. The figures around you are majestic and their appearance has an old-fashioned elegance. But the details, even ridiculous, have a sovereign value. You hear music coming from neighboring rooms in gusts, from an opera of genius is which human anguish and joy are summarized. However, you are not without anxiety. A mystery hovers. You look furtively at the hems of dresses with Watteau pleats with the apprehension of seeing a cloven foot.

"It is a true demon that is haunting you, but what a marvelous demon! You believe that no initiation is more profound. The soul, if only in illusion, is open to sensations of intense life, and by means of its almost infinitely increased faculty of imagination, sees things in a new light. It moves through the world with the intuition of unsuspected relationships. And curiosity awakes, which counsels going toward that unknown. Is not lack of energy often, perhaps even always, the consequence of the lack of interest that one finds in existence and its manifestations. One can, with the occult aid of bizarre gods, acquire the habit of activity. The ecstasy of certain hours reveals to our minds sudden and magical verities in the real meaning of the word.

"But that is sufficient. You have interrogated me. It was a nocturnal conference. Here is the morning, which will dissipate the clouds in which our conversation has gone astray."

They emerged from the smoky room, which had become livid by contrast with the frank clarity outside. On the sidewalk, an exquisite torpor gripped them. They went around piles of vegetables and roses. A few groups of noctambulists, in the middle of the street, were buying flowers. Ragged individuals with sly smiles awaited sous that had gone astray. The life of the day woke up to the din of carts. And there was an impression of moving through perfumes, under the oblique gaze of the rising sun, with the elastic fatigue of a happy night of insomnia, toward the refreshment of repose.

IV. Nightmares

The mere idea of a poison often produces the same effects as the poison itself. It is one of the powers of idea and an indication of one of its relationships with matter. Experience has vulgarized that doctrine, and suggestion, the study of which has entered the scientific domain, gives proofs of it every day. The theories exposed by Corbus haunted the mid of his interlocutor for long hours. Incapable of working, he tried in vain to sleep, in order to calm a strange overexcitement. The days went by slowly. Heavy clouds passed over the narrow street, darkening it at intervals, and the windows that Jean Derève could see opposite his own were more mysterious than ever.

He was aware of the indefinable attraction of mirrors, those enigmatic gaps open to the existence of thousands of phantoms that respire around us. How haunting it is to think of all those animate forms moving, all the way to the horizon, behind doors, walls, streets, with cries and gestures that overlap, appeal to one another and respond, and comprise a supple mantle of humankind over the vast earth! And each of those forms has its interior life and its intimacy, similar to ours, and also different from it.

An almost culpable curiosity carries the eyes of an observer toward the detail of the neighboring interiors perceived. The corner of an item of furniture, a painting on the wall, and a lamp on a table, have stories to tell. The vague soul of objects retrains the memory of presences and frictions. A silhouette passes the bay of the window or behind the curtains of the closed casement. Petty concerns and preoccupations are revealed, sometimes ridiculous, sometimes suggestive of emotion, sometimes confessing the profound resignation and in-difference that is the soul of objects, animals and the majority of humans. Some humans, like the others, re-main in the same place, with a few oscillations, and are never astonished; the succession of the minutes is for them a normal game.

The interiors divined, which the curtains or window panes hide from the gaze of the observer, are more for-tunate for the dream. One can conjecture them, and give free rein to the fantasy, certain that one is elsewhere and that no creation of our thought can fail to be realized in advance somewhere. The world, that of ideas like that of bodies, is unlimited in all directions, and in all the mean-ings of those directions.

Jean Derève's wandering gaze crossed the street and rose up as far as the balconies of the upper floors. He clung, in imagination, on to the narrow margins of the balustrades, with the fear of falling, experiencing the real sensation of his efforts, and then feeling his fingers quitting the stone, and his body plunging on to the piti-less sidewalk. Then, suddenly, breathing deeply, he found himself sitting in the ground-floor room again, with the solid floor beneath his feet.

All the familiar objects, the contemporaries and witnesses of his bizarre life, seemed to be congratulating him for having escaped the danger.

It was a sensation analogous the one that is experi-enced in a dream when one believes that one has fallen from a height. But in the dream, one always wakes up before reaching the ground, for if the illusion went as far as that, the cerebral shock would be such that one would surely die. Many sudden unexplained deaths during sleep are undoubtedly caused by a mortal dream that is not interrupted.

As a child, Jean Derève had supposed that the uniform earth could not extend without limits, and that one would arrive at the end of the world somewhere. The concept of an immense globe, the center of which was below and all the circumference above, did not enter his mind, any more than the minds of all other beings naïve by virtue of age of want of cultivation. Cosmogonies corresponding to that state of soul still exist. Savage humans believe that the world is a vast round surface borne on a circular ocean or on the void. That is the science of Homer. Why not? We smile at those primitive conceptions, but either progress is only a vain word—and which of our scholars would accept that hypothesis?—or they must admit that one day, their explanation of the universe as they see it today will appear as ingenuous and false as those of Ptolemy or the Hindus. It is necessary that discovered verities are transformed into errors in order to give birth to other verities. All forms disappear in their turn.

But this is the present form: in space there is no up or down. Without that, one could fall of the edge of the earth. We would be like Victor Hugo's Satan, falling from heaven for all eternity. On the contrary, for someone who knows the laws of attraction, is it not more amusing to imagine, an undeniable fact, that the approach of a more voluminous heavenly body, surging from the depths of the abyss at our zenith, would invert the natural law, and would cause to appear above our heads the ground on to which we would have to fall, the earth, without having moved, suddenly being found above us, with its houses overturned and its roofs hanging!

Before mental anxieties, such questions had troubled his soul. In the early days of childhood, he had been gripped by mystery, spiritual or material. There are people who are carried away at birth by a fay, perhaps wicked, but whose smile is persuasive, in order to imprison them in the prison of enchantments. What a mortal rose thought is! And what suffering those whom its perfume intoxicates endure! Their sentimentality, like their reflection, is exasperated by impacts that are too numerous and too different. That astonishment of life, like a new wine, sometimes lasts for many years; and their intelligence is only a glimmer sheltered from the wind by the hollow of a hand, which does not prevent them from bumping into some wall every three paces.

For there is no durable road; every idea that one follows to the end arrives at the absurd and the void. Fortunate are those philosophers who suppose that problems are resolved by the declaration that problems do not exist! More fortunate are those who, with a light heart, gladly accept antinomies and rejoice in being able to affirm the contrary of everything, which proves that verities are numerous, and who work untiringly to construct the temple of their ignorance, sustained by columns that are alternately black or white, extracting great hope from that diversity of color for the solidity of the edifice! Even more fortunate, finally, are those who, without adopting a fine title, renounce inventing systems and accommodate themselves, in order to live, to a few appearances of verity that the crowd passes from hand to hand like false coins whose circulation is urgent.

Assuredly, the best thing is to believe that they are all made of proven gold and to content oneself with them for the purchase of the petty joys that distract us sufficiently from dawn to nightfall. One builds one's house

of planks or heaped stones; a fortuitous sculpture orna-
ments its façade in places, A few temple ruins are the
edifice for wellbeing. It is necessary to accept life without interrogating it and avoid thought with jealous care.
Anyway, what proof is there that thought is not a disease
of matter, as a pearl is, in spite of its beauty?

It is therefore the duty of the legislator to proscribe
severely any attempt in the order of knowledge. Let us
recognize, in praise of that rational individual, that he
has always acquitted it. One tolerates metaphysicians,
old men who are slightly mad, who live in wretched at-
tics weaving fabrics that they believe to be solid with the
cobwebs tangled around their miserable hovel. They are
not dangerous. As well as their conceptions being far
apart from those commonly received, they also set themselves aside from the living forms by which they might
be seduced. They are content with their dream. They do
not find anyone who consents to realize it in the palpable
form of a book, and thus, there is an admirable order in
it. People only print conventional things; there is no fear
of new ideas circulating. Thus, a peril is avoided.

If younger and more ardent men, on the other hand,
decide to believe in the reality of their ideas, to explain
life by means of formulae not yet pronounced, and if
they have the audacity to go into public squares to announce what they believe to be the good word, they immediately become malefactors, for they overturn the
fragile order of received things. All sects rise up from
their pulpits of ignorance and dogmatize against them.
They are accused of having claimed that Caesar is not
Caesar and that the priests of the moment are the priests
of error. Ordinary men have never experienced the need
to ask whether the earth rotates. They rise up as if
against a personal insult if anyone preoccupies himself

with the earth and its rotations. Every spark of wisdom ignites a pyre. Every prophet who speaks on the mountain sees a cross erected nearby on the height.

Life can only subsist by virtue of insouciance. It is a conspiracy of sorts. At birth, we perceive next to our cradle the faces of saddened people, who put their fingers over their mouths to inform us of the law of silence. The human race is like a voyager walking alongside a gulf into which it is forbidden to look down for fear of being attracted by the depth. Nor can he raise his gaze toward the starry sky above his head, for the slightest false step might be fatal. And thus we proceed, attentive to the narrow strip of the path.

The mysterious links between the physical and the mental, between what we call our body and what we call our soul, imply that that image is not merely an image but the double expression of a verity. It is the fear and the love of the abyss that awakens great anxieties. The real Pascal, dissimilated by the entitled pamphleteer of Port-Royal,[13] lived in that terror, equally anxious at the edge of a bridge over the Seine and the brink of mathematical infinity. The body shares the apprehensions of the soul, under a more gripping form. Thoughts, like actions, refuse to lean over from the top of the tower.

---

[13] Blaise Pascal became the most prominent defender of the schools associated with the Cistercian Abbey of Port-Royal when they became associated with the reformist movement of Jansenism and attacked by the Jesuits. He probably contributed to *La Logique, ou l'art de penser*, the textbook produced at the Abbey for use in the schools., which became very popular because it was in French, at a time when most such texts were written in Latin.

That emotion was manifest in our individual without him having understood its meaning; but no one was more subject than him to vertigo. It is one of the impressions that all humans are susceptible of experiencing, at a given moment, like fear, but with a very different intensity. Some cannot consider the ground from a distance of a few meters without suffering it. Others climb scaffolding or go to place a flag on the spire of a cathedral with perfect tranquility. Only the imagination of such a height terrorizes. For a longtime he conjectured, with a laudable modesty, that that infirmity was only a sign of inaptitude to sublime ideas. But he reflected one day that the roofer who constructs the temple belfry and works on a fragile plank, might have base ideas. Such reasoning reassured him. For him, it was an immediate torture to lean out of a window. As one experiences an imperious desire to scratch an irritating wound, he leaned out, breathless, hanging on to the supporting bars, defying the formidable appeal, but without remembering having once forgotten, in the balcony of some apartment, to verify mechanically the solidity of the support.

A friend who sometimes welcomed him in his nocturnal excursions, at the other end of the city, who lived on the fifth floor, smiled on seeing him taking ridiculous and tragic precautions before going to sleep whenever he was given hospitality. He placed all the movable items of furniture before the windows of the room. One might have thought that he was barricading himself against space. He was haunted by the idea of waking up after an improbable fit of somnambulism, lying on the pavement of the street, his head fractured, respiring just enough to be aware that he was doomed.

And as happens to those who live, above all, by means of the imagination, all the following scenes of desolation unfurled before his eyes. He saw himself transported home, in the midst of a curious emotion. He witnessed his funeral. He was moved to pity by his death. He thought about the various impressions of those who knew him, and the fleeting sadness of his friends.

Curiously enough, in dreams—but who can find the law of dreams?—no such anxiety ever pursued him. The association of ideas is made there mechanically, without the control of reason. Human mentality, at those moments, can be regarded as similar to that of superior animals when awake. The absence of consciousness and reflection produces a different effect on joys and pains. The former seem more profound, their spontaneity not being spoiled by analysis. Pains, on the contrary, are less sharp and devoid of range. The impressions are brushed in a perpetual change. That vagabondage explains why the preoccupations of the day do not necessarily return by night. The mind is fatigued by them and does not persist.

That is so true that it is sometimes sufficient, in order to expel a redoubtable image from slumber, to think about it obstinately before going to sleep. It is even easier to represent to ourselves insignificant impressions that have passed during the day and whose trace was so light that by the evening we have forgotten them completely. But there is a marker that we have placed without knowing it, Some insignificant figure perceived during our excursions, which we scarcely glimpsed, will come back to haunt our sleep and take on an absurd and immeasurable prominence and importance.

One might even suppose that nocturnal sensations are complementary to those of the day. Thus, when one has considered a red disk for a long time, it is a green circle that one perceives with closed eyes. Heavy people dream that they have wings. The fantasy of Jean Derève, weary of vertigo, found the opposite torture in the shadow of the night. His nightmares were of believing himself to be immured alive in a tomb.

He knew the futile effort of trying to lift a stone that the gravedigger had posed solidly, and the terror of imagining the blue sky, the open air and the song of birds toward the sun, from which he was separated for eternity by heavy black earth. Or, alternatively, he had the illusion of waking up in a narrow and obscure tunnel and perceiving in the distance the light of a thin opening, toward which he tried desperately to crawl, through a passage that diminished with every one of his movements. He could no longer advance, held by the shoulders, nor did he want to go back, into the blackness. He choked, and woke up with frightened cries. But space only tormented him in his hours of lucidity.

His new ideas felt that preoccupation. One cannot emphasize enough how the special vision of life influences judgments and actions. Such an inadmissible dread, sometimes because of its ridiculousness, can turn existence in a definitive direction. Each of us has one of those insignificant traits in his character, which only has importance for oneself. They are bizarre and tyrannical demons, whose influence is always present.

Although sufficiently disposed to remain without lassitude in the same place, Jean Derève did not detest voyages, but he frequented the seaside. His ideal for his old age was a modest house on a Mediterranean shore, with the sun and the shade of a few parasol pines, for calm reveries to the monotonous sound of blue waves. Mountains would crush him with their mass if he lived at the foot, but, on the other hand, he would evidently have feared climbing their slopes with his cortege of phantoms, even to go and inscribe his name, with a patriotic emotion, on the summit of some Gaurisankar.

Chamois and izards appeared to him, by virtue of their aptitude, to be animals as fabulous as the chimera. He liked cats, but not for the somewhat banal sensuality of plunging his hand into a dusty and greasy fur. What he respected in them was the miraculous gift of walking over the roofs and the gutters of houses and having frightful falls without danger. The she-cat of one of his friends, which came to visit him, had fallen from the mansard where she lived several times without any damage. He conceived an admiration for her in consequence. The worship of the Egyptians seemed to him to be justified; but he did not experience any desire to tread the summits of the pyramids with a triumphant foot.

He did not even venture into elevators willingly. Apart from the fact that those instruments appeared to him to be constructed in a barbaric fashion, and to present perpetual dangers by virtue of their complication, he could not abide the impression of sensing the void increasing beneath him. All of his heroic memories were of climbs inside monuments or walks on roads separated from a precipice by guard-rails.

He had never risked himself in the nacelle of a balloon. What folly to believe in the possible conquest of the air! Some things are realizable, *a priori*, although not yet realized, but others are not. Humans are made to live in the ground and maintain the maternal contact that gives them strength, like Antaeus. They are no more independent of the native soil than vegetables. After a brief excursion, they return beneath it. Meanwhile, the conformation of the body, although one accords some credit to the law of adaptation, cannot lend itself to flight. It is impossible to sustain oneself in the air other than by accident and by artificial means.

Humans, conquering the air, will always dread a fall; they will never equal the birds, any more than divers or temporarily submerged swimmers are really fish. The latter, in any case, cannot go beyond a few meters into the profundity of the seas; and humans cannot rise beyond the inferior layers of the atmosphere. They will never know the monsters that glide silently over the obscure sand of the oceans, any more than the great birds, masters of the air, whose very shadows do not reach as far as us. The successive planes of matter cannot be penetrated.

Literature and art furnish a pretext for similar opinions. The Tarpeian rock and the gulf into which the Spartans hurled deformed children are celebrated in memory. Suspended with the arch-priest from the edge of the towers of Notre-Dame, breathlessly,[14] he saw the convulsed face of the soon-to-be cadaver, fingernails scraping the stone, dragged down by the invisible and implacable hands of gravity.

Is it not permissible, however, and this would be the greater mystery, to suppose that a fall from a great height ought to have the tragic terror that one apprehends? Everything exaggerated is attenuated or suppressed, and the faculty of suffering has narrower limits than one is accustomed to imagine. It is the same with all mortal things as with death, on which successive generations put a ridiculous mask, but which is nothing but a shadow, which is nothing. Once launched into the abyss, one loses the notion of the real. Have not voyagers related, having returned by a miracle from some accident on the

---

[14] While reading Victor Hugo's *Notre-Dame de Paris*.

side of a mountain, that they experienced an indefinable voluptuousness in feeling themselves floating in space? It is an illusion dearly paid for, immediately, to be freed for a second from the bonds of gravity. Might not the time that goes by, rapidly, before the definitive impact, by virtue of an eternal contrast, be overflowing with physical joy? Other examples of the same compensation present themselves to obscene minds that praise death by hanging. There is, surely, in the attraction that is the property of vertigo, a mysterious appeal, explicable by some reason as unknown as it is unexpected.

In any case, that kind of trespass has something that solicits, alongside the known horror. It is grandiose to launch oneself majestically into eternity. Some Emperor—was it not Heliogabalus, priest of the Sun?—had a tower constructed paved at the base with precious stones, for a pompous suicide.[15] That supposed in the Caesar in question a conception of life and death far from banal. He had a sense of decorum, and applied himself to rendering the insouciant unknown a slave. It is known that a soldier devoid of artistry prevented him from realizing his dream by murdering him ignominiously. That promptitude was unfortunate; it deprived us of a good example. But one imagines that the gems and enamels, skillfully enlaced in a mosaic, must have fig-

---

[15] The author is probably remembering a story by Catulle Mendès, "L'Empereur et les papillons" (tr. as "The Emperor and the Butterflies"), in which such a tower is constructed. The much-slandered Elagabalus, whose name was transformed by historians into Heliogabalus, was only eighteen years old when he was murdered, having become a puppet emperor at fifteen, and is highly unlikely to have been the monster of depravity portrayed in propagandistic writings.

ured in advance the veritable bloodstains by which they were splashed.

It is the most elegant death, the prompt return to the earth from which humans have emerged. It is astonishing that the moderns have forsaken the ancient gesture. One does not find traces of it even in the practices of the comfortable clubs that gather together the lovers of suicide, in America or elsewhere. The revolver is not infallible and seems too administrative. There is no senior bureaucrat that does not have one in his drawer. Poison, in general, causes suffering. The leap into a river might seem to approach the form that occupies us, but it is the drowning rather than the fall that one seeks.

Traditions fade away. Such forgetfulness can only be explained by the ever-increasing ignorance of decency and natural laws. Organized barbarity makes progress every day. One does not even know any longer how to take one's leave. Suicides from high towers displease the people down below. About once a year some unhappy conservative jumps from the Arc de Triomphe, but the purity of the act is always spoiled by a sort of patriotic memory. Provincial notaries climb the interior steps of the edifice thinking about Napoléon and saluting their last sun like that of Waterloo. All men of taste experience an embarrassment at that observation, a slight but painful sentiment of the ridiculous.

For it is necessary not to profane rites. The fear of the abyss and the fatal desire to fall into it surely have a profound origin. The law of gravity governs the entire realm of matter. It has for correspondence in the spiritual world amour. It is the most mysterious and the most universal of laws. One cannot see it as anything other than a tendency to unity.

By the same reasoning, the custom of burying the dead appears just. The pyre is only a simulacrum. The smoke does not escape gravity. Barbaric and devoid of logic are the people among whom cadavers are exposed in the branches of trees or near to the nests of vultures. It is true that tomorrow, the branches are transformed into humus and that the vultures, after their death, will end up in the ditch, but burial respects the return more promptly, and allows a better understanding of the scant importance that the individual has. Humans return to the earth, as waves, having surged forth momentarily, fall back into the ocean.

After a day of vagabondage along metaphysical paths, Jean Derève reposed, determined to follow until the extreme the visions that the previous night had summoned to his brain. His state of soul appeared to hum to be appropriate to the most moving suggestions. In any case, it was only in slumber that he felt that he was in full possession of his imaginative faculty. How fortunate one would be if one had the power to express immediately what one experiences at those moments of absolute spirituality in which space and time are transformed!

During the day, the fatigues and the constraint of the body inhibit the play of thought; but the night is favorable to the appearance of astral forms, to the advent of messengers sent by the Beyond. There is no longer any absurdity in the enchainment of theories that appear the most strange viewed with the inadequate clarity of diurnal reasoning, Night inspires sibyls and lovers.

He favored the blooming of unusual flowers himself. Magic is made of precautions. Nothing of his repose and its accessories was left to chance. He consulted Apollonius of Tyana learnedly. And, certain of seeing interesting things, he enveloped his body, and especially his head, in the white woolen cloth that infallibly provokes evocations.

It is an ancient custom that was lost and rediscovered. The flamen of Jupiter wore a woolen bonnet, later reduced to a plume of the same substance, which only had a figurative meaning, but men of images surround their head with their cloaks in order to deliver themselves to meditations. The flamen of Jupiter conserved the sacred fire in his house. Jean Derève knew that the sacred fire in question was retained in the shelter of a veil, and that thought too is a fragile gleam that needs to be protected and prevented from being dispersed by any wind. In addition, the most recent scientific discoveries permit seeing the brain as a real source of energy that is externally manifest in certain cases by phenomena of light and heat.

He had a dream.

In consequence of some fall, or some departure from life, his soul and his body found themselves in the inferior world of the caverns in which the vulgar suppose the existence of gnomes, guardian of subterranean treasures. It might be the case that Heaven, or at least what we call by that name, the goal of our aspirations, is, in reality, beneath us. That hypothesis would be favored by worshipers of fire, since the closest fire, the one that can naturally guide us toward the most distant, is situated by geologists in the center of our globe, of which it is the heart. One could then consider successive humankinds, living one above another, as becoming more perfect as they occupy a circle more interior—in contrast to the Inferno of Dante, devoid of the diminution of the spheres—all the way to the material annihilation of the hearth, being an obstacle to their existence. One admits readily that it is at the summit, the vanishing point of the lines, that the pyramid, for example, has all its reality.

At what depth was the land to which the sleeper saw himself transported? He could not take account of it, not having had the sensation either of the departure or of traveling; or perhaps he had forgotten the passage from exterior life to this one. But already, space was becoming, in one sense, exceedingly limited. This habitable world was, in breadth, similar to the galleries that coal miners hollow out, the height of which is measured by that of a man. A different existence unfurls on a determined plane. But roads, in places headed toward distant dwellings, forming crushed crossroads. To the walls, at intervals, metal lamps were fixed, the vague glow of which illuminated a few meters of the road. And from black cavities in the wall, confusedly distinguishable by virtue of their darker stain, the murmur of speech escaped, as if the people of the realm were hiding in their houses for fear of even a dubious light. Those houses must have resembled tombs, and the life that went by there as grave and bleak as that of the buried dead undoubtedly is, beneath the sunlit earth.

At least the dreamer experienced, as soon as he took his first steps, a singular impression of liberation and security. His diurnal dreads were abolished, and the emotion that he felt, derived from the unusual situation, had nothing in common with the habitual haunting. Immured in a catacomb vaster and more definitive than the hypogea of Egypt, he could be apprehensive of everything, but he no longer dreaded falling, having he ground above him. Sometimes, however, at certain passages, when he raised his head, he was surprised and troubled, as if by a vertigo in reverse. Great gaping openings, as if sheerly sculpted, or produced by the explosion of a mine, appeared in the ceiling of the gallery. One might have thought them, by their irregular form, inverted abandoned quarries.

They plunged upwards for a few meters into the black rock, but had no issue, and one sensed all the thickness of the ground weighing upon them. A funereal bird, flying toward that illusion of space, fell back after three wing-beats, having touched the extremity of the hollow. They were doubtless the residues and marks of puerile attempts toward the Beyond, empty monuments of Icaruses who had tried in vain to flee. The only remaining results of those efforts were the heaps of debris on the floor beneath those passages, obstructing the route unnecessarily.

But that route became easier with habitude. A gradual slope became more accentuated; and he understood that the discovered country could not extend along a regular circumference, but must follow a spiral toward the nucleus. The law of progress was verified in this world as in others. The people who descended from the exterior experienced at every step a greater lightness, the slow and continual realization of equilibrium, and had to march toward the lower horizon as if toward liberation from odious weight. They circled, always approaching closer, around their ideal. What did it matter if the road became narrower with distance, and if they had to duck their heads in order to cross the threshold of the mystery? They would straighten up soon, in the unreal country outside time and space, with the liberty conquered from the heavy laws of this world.

His attention was attracted, while he went, by other gleams than those of the lamps, agitating in the depths of obscurities. One might have thought that they were torches carried by hands. The inhabitants of the subterranean region fled, frightened, as he approached, like humans at the sight of a celestial monster descending toward them. No sound could any longer be heard behind the walls, except that of stifled respirations. The audacity of the explorer did not go as far as the gesture of leaning his head or extending his hand toward the black openings of windows. He did not want to know, with a mortal frisson what shadowy gripping hand might seize his own as he held it out.

But he went on, insensible to the fear of such an adventure; or, rather, so profoundly plunged in an ocean of fear that all his senses were submerged. He perceived altars at the crossroads hollowed out in the walls, around which other lamps burned. His curiosity was solicited by the form of the idols, but the cavities were closed by narrow grilles and the depths of the retreats seemed to be too distant for anything whatsoever to be distinguished. His eyes were scarcely caressed by a vague golden reflection on the pleat of a garment. He did not know, and never knew subsequently, what Hecate was worshiped among those infernal peoples.

Undoubtedly he was traversing a city. Other familiar signs denounced the presence of a humankind; for all of them are similar in all the spheres and have the same known movements. Poorly extinguished embers against a boundary marker revealed a recent fire. Elsewhere, wreaths of sad flowers, placed on silent thresholds, enabled the supposition of a lugubrious celebration, or perhaps marked the door of a tomb within the tomb.

And there was the sensation of a march that became more rapid at every step. The slope had increased and the ground was fleeing, but without giving any other impression than still being equally reliable.

The silence was troubled. The voyager perceived a kind of murmur issuing from a distant gallery. He listened. Was he finally about to hear voices and know the language of the dead? The noise increased gradually. A cry rose up, which became several. The obscurity was colored by a diffuse light, which grew or was attenuated, as if by the sinuosities of a path; but every time the light returned more brightly and the noises more intense. And as the road opened on another, broader, the voyager scarcely had time, by means of an instinctive recoil, to take refuge in a shadowed corner. A crowd arrived upon him, so close that he could touch their garments. By the light of a hundred torches, uttering moans and howls, a disorderly troop surged forth of lugubrious men and women, the inhabitants of the black land.

They were all those individuals that a fatal attraction or some insupportable despair had precipitated into death. They were all those who had fallen from houses, towers and tall trees toward the formidable kiss of the earth, or from the height of rocks into the sea. Old men and children, leaning on crutches, let their twisted limbs dangle. Wretches with broken vertebral columns, folded in two, seemed to be defying the sky with the ridiculous stance of disarticulated puppets. They were all those who, on a moonless night, wandering through the countryside, had not seen the gulf opening under their feet, and had groped in the sudden void. The heads were wrapped in bandages from which blood was seeping in large patches, red and creamy. For it is on the head that the unfortunate fall, and the man summoned by the abyss rotates to hit the ground in accordance with his center of gravity.

As the funereal procession unfurled, terrifying faces were discernible in the play of obscure torchlight. Sometimes, two thin convulsed lips retained the heroism of the supreme resolution. Sad mothers passed by, their hair scattered, clasping shreds of bruised flesh to their hearts, the children with whom they had leapt from the top of walls on the day that a city was taken, having hidden them in order to conceal them from visible death in a fold of their cloak.

And all the madmen, all the inventors, all the Icaruses with broken shoulders, vain challengers of vertigo, went along the somber road toward the goal toward which the first prodigious leap had launched them. The most desolate trailed long black broken wings behind them. And the frightful canticle that rose from that crowd was made of every cry, howl of joy or clamor of unique distress uttered by each of them when they fell.

Jean Derève too uttered a cry of anguish, which woke him up, and of which he heard the prolongation in the night, even after having emerged from the tragic shadows of slumber.

The vibrant sensation was perpetuated. Then there was an ample and profound sigh, for the return to peaceful existence and repose in his bed, still seeing outlined among the vague flowers of the wallpaper, by the glimmer of the nightlight, crippled arms and bodies, hallucinated faces and split heads bursting like ripe pomegranates.

Then the fever finally calmed down. An immense lassitude invaded him. And gradually, without being aware of it, he fell back into unconsciousness and dream.

It was another vision.

It appeared to him that he was sitting in the middle of an empty room, the walls of which were whitewashed. There was no visible trace of any other furniture than the chair he occupied. He was alone. As the light penetrated broadly through the opening in the wall in front of him, he conjectured that he was on the topmost floor. It must be a house like those one finds in the bosom of populous cities, with a stone ledge running along the façade and the sloping pans of windows on the wall that rose in a mansard toward the roof. But the bay that extended transparently in front of him, as broad as it as high, was almost straight, with large thin iron crosses dividing the vast casements. And surely the winter months had come, for the light that designed its dream reflection on the floor was falling from the cold moon. In spite of the silence and the solitude, he knew that other existences were hidden around him, behind the partitions, like mute breaths spying on his own in the shadow of bleak fireplaces, near balconies with wrought iron bars.

How long had he been there now, and for what reason? He did not know, as one does not know, in dreams, the most logical things, and does not even ask oneself. Perhaps for years, as a consequence of circumstances recovering the details of which would have wearied his memory in vain; but his heart was oppressed and his soul was tormented by an indefinable anxiety. The distant corners of the room were lost in obscurity. All the tragic and future interest of the satiation was concentrated in the middle, in the terribly calm square of light in which the chair was placed. And on the other side of the narrow street, separated from him by the abyss, at the top of the house opposite, he saw a window that seemed to be the double of the one placed in front of him.

He thought that he suddenly perceived a movement in that other room. The windows opposite opened and a human form appeared. It was a woman clad in white. She was bare-headed, and her black hair was falling loosely over her shoulders. The pleats of her dress descended harmoniously all the way to the floor, tightened at her supple waist by a narrow belt.

The woman ought to have been beautiful, but the charm of the face vanished. Nothing was legible in her features but an expression of slight anguish and solemn resolution. Her lips shifted as if to pronounce some mysterious formula in a whisper. She was standing upright on the façade, her eyes upraised and lost, her feet at the level of the window. Then she opened her arms in a cross and, in a regular curve, leaned forward and allowed herself to fall

The seer made a gesture of alarm and, reproaching himself for his nonchalant stupor, ran toward the door and the staircase. Never had the steps seemed so numerous. He had the impression of passing an infinity of floors.

Finally, he reached the flagstones of the ground floor, but could not get out. All the inhabitants of the house, already descended, were packed in the corridor, and the threshold was obstructed by a curious crowd, with the same ecstatic and somber faces. Exclamations and proud sighs could be heard all around. The sound of ringing bells came from afar, which might as easily have been a festival carillon as a knell. It was permissible to conjecture, in accordance with the conversations, that a noble and ritual action had just been accomplished.

The witness of that strange scene finally succeeded in fraying a passage through the groups; and when the crowd had dispersed to some extent the street allowed the sight of forms in a pious attitude, all heading in the same direction. They appeared to be moving in the wake of a cortege, the prayers of which were still audible, borne in gusts by the wind, and the torches of which were snaking out there in the distance.

A few paces away, veiled women, snatching away their veils, were collecting, with respectful gestures, the blood of which a large pool reddened the ground.

One might have thought that the faithful were coming in the name of a bizarre religion to venerate some martyr dead for that religion.

And Jean Derève, finally, woke up completely, upset by the images that had been placed before his eyes.

He tried to find a logical link between the two scenes that had appeared. Was not the second, in a mysterious inversion, the prelude and the cause of the other? That woman had adored vertigo, and doubtless she had already joined the lugubrious procession of the inferior world. She was marching, as a shade, toward the weightless center.

And the idea came to him of a future religion with simple and terrible ceremonies. The science of ancient days had initially dressed the sacred forms. People adored Zeus, like Athene, before knowing what thunder was, and before knowing what lightning was. Science followed religion. Why not suppose, on the contrary, a religion born of science? Did not the theory of universal attraction, the most admirable of modern times, have sufficient beauty to be divinized, while awaiting a new progress of human thought to overturn that theory and find another formula of the universe? Could it not, in the meantime, also count its martyrs and its fanatics? And undoubtedly, one day, women would be seen adorned for the sacrifice, precipitated by the hands of the priest from the top of the temple and the tower, toward the sovereign Moloch.

That thought made him smile, but he thought that all religions have similar origins, inspired by fear or astonishment. And he discovered in that one, while playing with his visions, a profound and harmonious meaning.

Is not death divine, and is it not the only road to go toward God? It is from death that life is born, in a perpetual exchange. Blood streams and flame is an indefatigable movement. The creative force destroys forms and renews them. It separates in order to reunite. It is necessary to draw away incessantly from the heart of the world in order to return there.

Sunlight entered the room, dispersing nocturnal dread. Jean Derève remained extended, his head supported by the pillow. A sunbeam fell on a crimson curtain in front of him and made the color shine. He remembered the sacred fire, and the pool of blood at the bottom of the mortuary house.

And he knew that life is red.

V. The Magical Conversation

That evening, Jean Derève welcomed his friends. He took pleasure in exchanging impressions with them suggested by his recent experiences. Life, too long bleak and devoid of a goal was beginning to appear different to him. The meaning of the ceremonies that he had witnessed was gradually becoming clear. Whatever the procedure was, whatever the path followed, there is no joy more intense and more reliable than that of knowledge: suspecting the answer to life, examining all things, effortlessly, by the light of a sovereign idea; grasping the relationships and the laws, and realizing in oneself the accord and verity of the law. As soon as one glimpses the route, one smiles with confidence at the goal that one divines to be near henceforth.

Lucia presided over the gathering. A meal was the pretext. To the young woman's right Saint-Maur was seated, to her left Mathias Corbus. Jean Derève closed the square. Following the precept of antiquity, they were more numerous than the Graces and fewer than the Muses. The number four appears the best for a conversation that wants to remain general. It can also divide into duality. But, dialogue sometimes leading to monotony, it is appropriate that another interlocutor mingles with the exchange of words. Thus, the last of the witnesses, whoever that might be, by turns, can remain silent.

If the philosophy of Edgar Poe on furniture is not vain, the interior was laudable. The seats had a form combining style and comfort; the former always accompanies the latter to an extent. The room was illuminated by candles on the table emerging from light candlesticks, slightly tormented, with violets at their feet, like a tribute of flowers to the light; Jean Derève thought that a delicate Epicureanism exists. Plato's banquet appeared to him to be superior to a quarrel of dusty scholars in the depths of a library. Even serious ideas gain from being expressed in the presence of a feminine smile and before charming lips, even if they do not respond.

Charming lips should never speak. They ought only to know the idiom of the gods. One day, the only word will be the kiss.

The Amphitryon had just said grace. He had thanked his friends for having come.

"I regret," Saint-Maur hazarded, "that we are not seven or nine. I have nothing serious for which to reproach the number four, but I find it too square and, for that reason, too material. All numbers, I agree, are sacred, but seven and nine have more value. They design superior realities. The pentagram, for its part, does not lack merit. There are many excellent things that are fivefold."

Mathias Corbus replied: "You should consider that we ought to be counted not as four but as three and one. I'm expressing myself a little heavily. It's the style for demonstrations. Thus, we form a trinity submissive to the unity of Lucia. I'd develop that image if I had the leisure."

"It's a metaphysical madrigal," Saint-Maur explained

"And it's also a verity," said Corbus. "I'm astonished that no poet has thought of celebrating in lyric terms the beauty of numbers and their virtue. It should certainly be lamented. Pythagoras, without a doubt, must have written that poem, for he was something other than a calculator. I know that he adored numbers, those mysterious divinities without which it is not permitted to suppose the existence of anything whatsoever. But his works are lost and we only have, today, the metaphysics of genius. Men who know how to write no longer know how to philosophize.

"I can see the sage, on a clear Italian night, on the sea shore. Behind him and the curtain of trees, the white columns of his institute appear confusedly. Their air has a blue limpidity, and Pythagoras is contemplating the motionless stars. He is trying to read the number or the phrase that they trace in the firmament. The nocturnal silence has its profound eloquence. The gods wake up incessantly. How I would have liked to penetrate the sanctuary of Crotona! Doubtless the exterior walls were dressed with images reproducing the multiple forms of mortal life. One saw thereon combats at the gates of cities and warriors in glittering armor amid the rearing of horses. Alongside, an idyll was depicted; shepherds causing doves to fly way in a boscage. Meanwhile, on the wall shaded by the portico, closer to the entrance, a procession of musiciennes in long robes unfurled. They were singing, to judge by their mute but continual attitude, a hymn to the glory of the number that their action realized.

"Let us go in. The vault of the temple recalls, naturally, that of the heavens. On the interior columns, sumptuous letters of black cloth, as tall as a man, bear the silver lines of the symbols of immortality. But at the back of the choir stand images of the gods. They are simple and terrible. There are the triangle and the pentagram. There is the decad, mother of numbers. The back of the temple is, moreover, merely a curtain, somber in color, veiling for the profane as for the priest the supreme form, inexpressible by a form, the unity. In the middle of the nave, on an altar with three faces, the sacred fire burns night and day. It rises in a red triangle. Is base is a duality toward the divine encounter on high."

Saint-Maur slowly poured out the contents of a dusty bottle. Gleams shone through the crimson transparent wine.

"I raise my cup," he proposed, "in honor of Pythagoras. And I am a devotee of numbers. I don't know whether they have a magic and creative power. Perhaps they are the reality—I ought to say, one of the realities. I attribute a magical power to them because they represent harmonies and laws to us. We are certain that they are true, of the unknown as of the known, and since eternity."

"It's necessary," replied Mathias, "to be persuaded of that. And don't be astonished by the importance that the seekers of the occult have given to numbers at all times. They are still the simplest ideas to represent. Their language is universal; it is comprehensible in all the others. Each of the words that compose it can have an infinite meaning. Numbers are the key to the sciences, and to science. Don't find it strange that they preside over research in magic. It's a vast field of study, but the knowledge of numbers is invaluable to penetrate it. Let no one enter, said the philosopher, if he does not know geometry."

"Each of us," said Jean Derève, "has his idea and his tendency. You see magic everywhere."

"Where would it not be, if one understands the word? For it's only a matter of agreement. Perhaps what I call magic passes for you under another name, for the principle of the universe. Do you search in magical works for stories of sorcery? Do you think that the sacred books are a collection of incomprehensible formulae for knotting needles or casting spells? I am as careless of that science as of an old coin of the time of Caesar. But magic is the science of relations and logic, imperfectly known, which is in everything that exists. There is a law, of which we sometimes decipher an isolated word. A sage is a man who succeeds in reading an entire phrase. God, if he exists, can read the entire book, and knows all the harmonies, which probably express a unique word.

"Everything is connected. When astrologers tell you that every existence is submissive to the influence of a planet, they are only applying the universal principle to the particular. In return, the simplest of our actions influences the march of the universe. Renan was mistaken when, with a smile, he enunciated scorn for our vain agitations: 'What can that do to Sirius?' I know that the progress of an ant in a lost corner of the earth is in a relationship of influence with the revolutions of Sirius. Every step we take displaces the globe beneath our feet. It draws away or approaches us, alternately, in the measure and proportion of its mass with ours. Doubtless that movement is lost in an infinity of others, but it is an element therein. Everything is at the center of everything. Nothing is isolated. Every atom is caught in the formidable network of the immensity. And we, more than the ancient peoples, ought to fear when we raise our heads that we might break the vault of celestial crystal that envelops us everywhere.

"But it is not only the material laws that it is important to conceive. There are more important relationships. The undulation of our gestures being perpetuated to infinity, each of us can, at the precise moment, create the world anew. An act of will, like a gesture, lasts forever. The redoubtable gift of creation is in every created thought. To know those occult connections, the fraternity of beings in the universal harmony, is the goal of magic. And it is not in vain that occultists take as a symbol and a seal the star with five branches, the pentagram. The star radiates in all directions and the lines of each triangle go toward infinity."

"Those are fortunate speculations," Jean Derève objected. "I can admit that magic is the universal science in which all the others die away like waves in the sea, but a science supposes books and means of investigation. We will not always have, as at present, prophets among us."

"If you read the works," said Saint-Maur, "you would probably be put off. They're incomprehensible or puerile. We have not realized the slightest progress since the almanacs of Albertus Magnus. But ought magic to be a pretext for vulgarization? I doubt that there are authors that one can read without preliminary study, I even doubt that it is necessary to read any particular author. Of all the sciences, it is the most personal to realize. If you request counsel, it ought not to be from anyone but yourself. No one is qualified to direct you. Éliphas Lévi announces to you on every page that a mystery is about to be revealed, and then stops, doubtless fearing to have said too much. Reading him produces the effect on me of an excursion in a fiacre, in which one has the illusion at every minute that one is about to depart at a gallop."

"The comparison is not flattering to the mage," said Lucia, "But I've read his books. He's a sly defrocked priest. He has, moreover, the excessively desolate air of no longer running the risk, in our epoch, of being burned."

Mathias Corbus shook his head. "It's necessary not to exaggerate. The vanity of theoreticians is always evident, but a few interesting notes can be found in that

123

one. Let us praise him for not having sacrificed too much to the love of fancy dress. All the ceremonial of magical evocations is indicated at length in the pages of his ritual, but ceremonies are necessary. The flaming sword, the cup and the trident have a utility that is not what you might believe. The value of talismans, a representative value, ought no more to be denied than that of gold. It's necessary to refrain, however, from falling into ridiculous excess and multiplying images unnecessarily.

"I will say as much about the formulae and the literature appropriate to the celebrations of the unknown god. The invocations that are addressed to the mysterious powers might have a meaning that escapes us. Let us also refrain from another excess, but let us not refuse to recognize the influence of rhythm on thought. All the announcers of oracles were originally poets too. The golden verses of Pythagoras, which are attributed to him falsely, would not have reached us if they had not been verses. Nothing, strictly speaking, opposes magic, like Roman history, being put into madrigals."

"I know magical verses," sighed Saint-Maur. "They're very bad. Stanislas de Guaita, to speak only of the dead, is a pitiful poet. He has disciples who give evidence of a great originality in addressing prayers to Sathan with an *h*.[16] It's the devil's tail of magic. I understand that someone might be put off if he commences his studies with ridiculous works devoid of science, good taste and good faith. It's only necessary to read the old classics, unfortunately difficult to procure, not to mention the obscurities they contain, even for educated readers."

---

[16] As in *Les Noces de Sathan, drame ésotérique* (1892) by Jules Bois.

"I grant you all those difficulties," replied Corbus. "We have no comfortable guide for good wills and debutants. A few summaries exist, which summarize one another. 'Summarize one another,' saith the Lord. It's a means of having ideas. However, if the literary blossoming corresponds to a preset preoccupation, no epoch has been as curious about the unknown. Our religions are reduced to external apparatus, and are dead. Only a rigid mantle, like a heavy golden cope, embroidered with images, keeps the cadaver upright. We are emerging from the sacred wood of yesteryear. In the plain that leads us to the next clump of blessed trees, the occult river flows invisibly. Abandoned marbles cover the moss behind us. Forgetfulness is falling over the past gods; the figure of the future gods still remains unknown. What does it matter, since they are both merely images? But mystery follows us to the next halt like a torch-bearer. If you try to interrogate him, I fear that he will only respond with the disappointing word: 'Seek.' There is no other formula. Timid men are discouraged and think that the great unknown would have done better, for the sake of justice, to reveal the supreme verity to us in clear terms. Others content themselves with conventional and dogmatic affirmations presented by systems elaborated completely by ingenious minds.

"The former and the latter alike are unaware that the solution to the problem is not outside but within us. It is a matter of knowing whether the thought inherent in the world is at its origin or in the future, whether creation was a unique act or is being realized every day. Perhaps the truth is found in the accord of the two verities, in the idea of the fall and the return. Humankind, descended from God, will be the future god. And progress will only exist by virtue of the development of consciousness toward self-knowledge, considered as a goal. It is in your soul and your heart that the only altar is erected at which the sacrifice ought to be celebrated. Books, even the most savant, are vain. Science is not exterior. Everyone ought to be his own initiator.

"If we say that magic, as we define it, summarizes all other studies, you can see that it is futile to search in works, in which only indications can be found. Mistrust those who claim to be able to teach you occult science, like English, in twenty lessons, You will not discover the word that transmutes metals into gold. Ali Baba's Sesame is only a symbol, albeit having, like any symbol, a value of hidden meaning. Nor does a phrase exist that, when pronounced, evokes the devil, apart from the fact that the devil does not exist. But there are secret laws by which one can direct one's thought and will. By putting ourselves in conscious harmony with the laws of life, we really could change metals into gold, for we would know the realities of those terms beneath the appearances and we would be able to play with the appearances before our eyes at will. We would also emerge victorious from the struggle against the devil—or, rather, the disorder that vocable represents. And everything would be for the best. We would be mages, without it being necessary to put on the red robe and constellated hat of magicians.

"The precepts of occult science are not so much precepts as counsels. They do not suppose a particular and fragmentary knowledge so much as the conquest of a state of soul. Let us open our eyes not upon books, but upon the mystery of life. Let us not listen to dead formulae but to murmurs and harmonies. Doubtless every science supposes a guide and elements, but it is not necessary, in order to be a sage, to speak Hebrew. The authors of occults treatises have fallen into the same error as the dialecticians of the Middle Ages, who reduced the art of reasoning to the knowledge of the syllogism and its sixty-four forms. Their scholasticism teaches the art of the multiple fashions of unreason. They have thrown the mantle of phrases over the nudity of thought.

"I think, therefore, that anyone who makes an exposé, by getting rid of all infantile apparatus, will realize a useful work, which might carry in its fecund womb the Great Work. Progress is not yet accomplished. After the arid works, we have had the variations of literature and art. All those writing about magic believe themselves lost to honor if they do it give in their turn a description of the Sabbat. They have remained at images. One shivers of seeing the goat of Mendes,[17] horns on the head and dugs on the breast, pensively seated on a throne around which the round-dance of witches and necromancers circles. How much simpler it would be to express the idea that the symbolic scene represents!

It is true that the young writers would lose a success of horror counted by them in advance, about which they care more than the discovery of the truth. It is the classic morsel that wins prizes. And the one who passes for the most profound mage is the one whose description causes the best shudder. That is because magic, like all the sci-

---

[17] The "goat of Mendes" was the name attributed by Éliphas Lévi to the famous image reproduced in his *Histoire de la magie* of the "Sabbat goat," sometimes also associated with the name "Baphomet" that occurs in the "confessions" extracted from Knights Templar by torture during Philippe le Bel's demonization of the Order. Lévi took the reference from an allegation by Herodotus that the inhabitants of Mendes— Djedet, a city in Egypt—was depicted with the head and legs of a goat. (Herodotus was mistaken, as usual; the deity particular to Djebet, Banebdjedet, actually had the head of a ram.)

ences, follows a law of evolution. It is still in the Romantic phase. No doubt it will give way to a more realistic science, which it is preparing, as alchemy anticipated chemistry. I fear, however, that the comparison is inexact, for chemistry and alchemy, both incomplete, will be united in a future synthesis.

I understand, to get back to it, that in the present epoch you are weary of rediscovering identical puerilities indefatigably. Even the interpretation of noble figures and symbols ought not always to have the same servility. A symbol only has the value that we give to it. If you produce a dissertation on numbers you will find hidden meanings therein different from those that someone else, Pythagoras, for example, found. The error would be to believe that Pythagoras, in expressing the formulae, never transmitted the meaning to us. If we summarize under the same sign other verities than his, we will have done better magical work than in trying to rediscover the principles that the sign represented for him. Formulae are an algebra for resolving the problems of life. The formula has been transmitted to us; it is up to us to give it meaning.

"You can argue as to whether or not the star of the pentagram does or does not represent the theoretical human being, with the head, the two arms and the legs, and whether the same sign, inverted, shows the face of the goat with the horns on top, but you would no more be a mage than an unintelligent but erudite grammarian. But another knows that all things need an image in order to be expressed. He will enclose his will in a formula, whatever it might be, and if he looks at that sign, rich in meaning that it recalls and summarizes, as a Christian looks at the cross, he will have presented all the energy of his will to it every time.

"The sign is like a focal point that gathers rays together. Do you think that the flag around which armed men gather has a value in itself? But it concentrates the audacity and courage of all of them in its folds. We have eyes in order to see, and mysterious conceptions ought to appear to our eyes. Our thought and our mental activity are supported on a material form, as Antaeus drew new strength every time he touched the ground. And the poet, without being aware of it, does the work of magic when, in order to write in her praise verses that are worthy of her, he evokes the absent face of the beloved. Would all the scattered thoughts and the visions haunting his mind come running faithfully to his impatient rendezvous, and would the sonorous words unite in a beautiful sequence, like a chain of golden rings, if some magical formula—her name for example—did not play the role of amalgamator? It is the value of all fetishes, pieces of wood or metal in which a hidden treasure is contained.

"We will accomplish miracles, in pronouncing a sacred appeal, even if that appeal is only sacred because it summarizes, once and for all, your energy and your will. It is necessary for you to succeed in believing that you will vanquish by that sign. Every time that, from then on, you have the sign in your presence, you will be sure of triumphing. For whoever knows the unlimited power of absolute confidence, it will seem quite extraordinary if you were not, in fact, victorious. I shall not even mention encounters in which success is uniquely in the idea, which are more numerous than is believed.

"But that is the whole of active magic. That theory appears to be the development of a banal proverb. It's a matter of taking the hackneyed axiom 'to want is to be able' in a more real and more profound sense. A word pronounced with certainty extends infinitely. And as nothing is isolated, following another important precept, it enchains and enslaves, more surely than the lamp or ring of Arabian tales, the occult powers that circulate around us."

Discreet applause saluted the orator's words. From then on the guests seemed to be in true magical communion. Lucia got up, picked up a few flowers from the table with a charming gesture, and, after weaving them into a makeshift crown, came to place it on the head of the man who was now silent. They all admired the grace of the movement, and Jean Derève made a eulogy to the light hands, comparing them to doves that had flown through the air carrying palms.

"In order to enlace with futile words those grave revelations, I will say what I think of hands, which are the body's wings. Is it because of their evident spirituality that painters have some difficulty depicting them in their paintings? But I know that the most skillful despair of it. Their attitude is impossible to fix. They always seem too heavy or too apparent; and I think that good artists avoid the difficulty by drawing them smaller than they really are. That's because in reality, they escape the gaze by virtue of their perpetual movement. It's therefore necessary, as soon as one wants to show them motionless—and it's the fault of the painter—to imitate their flight be refining them. Thus, the impression they produce, in spite of the momentary arrest, approaches the one to which we're accustomed."

All hands were agitated in a sign of assent. Lucia's had a rosy transparency in the candlelight. The cups circulated in the midst of a general conversation and a joyous abandon.

Then, once again, Corbus' voice was raised, seriously.

"What we've said about talismans is verified in a remarkable fashion. Since I received the crown I've had a true inspiration. And one could, at this moment, by virtue of the effect of that divine imposition or perhaps the generous wines that our Amphitryon has poured for us, believe in the prophetic Pythia. The seat where I am sitting is suddenly becoming a tripod, and I would experience a dolor if I were condemned to silence or if anyone refused to grant my words the value that I'm sure they have."

"We're all very disposed to listen to you," replied Jean Derève. "It's necessary, in all ceremonies, to choose a choirmaster. Your science has designated you. The presence of a charming form, which inspired you, would render us patient, in any case, to hear the strangest theories. This evening's are reasonable; I won't say a word against them. And I find it just to take as the departure point of the problem, the axiom you quoted on the power of the will. Do we know of what a man might be capable, what he can know and realize, as soon as he knows the laws of life? But I will attack that passionate question at the very foundation. If the science you extol is that of relationships as yet unknown, which resolve appearances, is it given to us only to modify appearances by our influence, or things in themselves? Humans have been seen at all times, marvelously endowed, accomplishing prodigies for the eyes of the amazed crowd. But what is there for the eyes? In other words, does the miracle exist objectively?"

"I believe I can say," said Saint-Maur, "that you're posing the question poorly. Your distinction between things as they are in themselves and as they are for us is vain. Nothing exists except for us. Don't even try to define matter, for example, apart from its relations with our

131

senses. What is matter and what is mind? It would be indispensable to respond, and you'll never be able respond until you ask yourself whether the mage is the master of matter or mind.

"All the difficulties of ancient philosophy come from that arbitrary distinction. There are not two essences but two modes. Extent and thought are only various manifestations—I scarcely dare to say different, even less, if I don't want to be absurd, opposite—of the same activity. But mind is that force at its maximum condensation; with the consequence that one could, by going as far as paradox, affirm that what is called mind is infinitely material. Admit, in order to explain all sorts of appearances, as many degrees as you wish.

"The solitaries of India realize prodigies that weak minds deny conveniently. By concentrating their attention on a seed planted in the earth, they can cause the plant to germinate after a time and to grow visibly under their gaze. But are they doing anything other than dispersing, in a material appearance, a vital force contained within them? Their mind changes into matter, the two being the same force, differently manifested.

"You have doubtless witnessed experiments in spiritism. You have seen, or people have told you that they have seen, flowers apported into a room, which come from outside. If you believe in the scholastic distinction between matter and mind, those facts are quite absurd. Flowers cannot pass through a wall. And how can other phenomena be explained, which are regarded as usual by all evocateurs? Apparitions of phantoms have occurred in all times. It is not necessary to go back to the pythoness of Endor.

"What is designated by the name of materialization is a habitual fact of magic. Suppose that the fluidic forms are decomposed and subtilized in order to reunite on the other side, in the presence of witnesses. Can you admit that the imprints left on wax, for example, which are those of a hand, were produced by substances more inconsistent than the wax? That would be to go against the most sanctified laws. I'm reasoning in accordance with facts that are not always proven—there is a great deal of charlatanism in magic—but it is sufficient that some are true.

"I'll go further and say that one can argue on the basis of the possible but never effectuated. It's only a matter of considering all substances, those that are regarded as spiritual or material, from a single point of view and departing from experience for conjecture.

"Consider, therefore, the various milieux, solid or fluid. You find it natural that a lead pellet creates a passage through a sheet of water without effort and without shattering. Now, everything is similar. You can imagine a substance sufficiently weak for a bubble of air to make a violent hole thought it similar to a cannonball flying through the air. Extend the comparisons and the reasoning, utilizing increasingly dense milieux. You can believe without contradiction that a substance exists in the same relationship of condensation to diamond as diamond has with water. A body of that substance would traverse a wall of diamond or steel as easily as a steel ball traverses water.

"It is thus that apparitions or phantoms circulate without effort and pass through walls. No door can stop them. It is not their vanity but, on the contrary, their extreme material reality that gives them that power. And if you're astonished that they escape contact with our senses, I'll respond that our senses are incapable of grasping what is too distant from their measure, at either end of the spectrum, the overly subtle as well as the excessively hard. Perhaps what we call fluid is not fluid enough for us. Whether a body passes through ours without dividing it, because of the great difference in density, or whether we pass through the body, the result is the same."

"Saint-Maur," said Mathias Corbus, "has just enunciated several verities. The idea of universal relativity is the most important of all. It is necessary to cease to believe, like the Hellenes, that the Peloponnese is the center of the world, and with all antiquity that the Earth is the center of the universe. Above all, it is necessary to refrain from applying to the rest of the world our personal conceptions and manner of seeing. How many infantile examples one could give of that cause of errors! I believe that astronomers, speaking of the temperature that reigns in interstellar space, suppose it to be eighty degrees Centigrade.[18] I ask what right they have to make that supposition. Perhaps they mean: the lowest temperature that humans have observed, marked by the lowering in a tube of terrestrial glass, of a drop of a liquid known to us, or a metal—it does not matter: to a certain degree. But in the same way that we do not now, in the scale of grandeur, which steps correspond to us—the stars on the one hand, and the infusoria on the other, limit the horizon for the senses—the degrees of the temperature scale are surely infinite in the order of what we call cold or warmth.

---

[18] This is an obvious mistake. The first estimate of the temperature of interplanetary space to be popularized in France was made by Fourier, but was amended by Charles Pouillet in 1838, on the basis of experiments carried out with an actinometer, to minus 142°C. That was still the widely accepted figure in 1904.

More reasonable scholars, already admit at the edge of the earth such a lowering of temperature that the air in its outermost layer might be frozen and solid; their theory, seductive and poetic, resuscitates the crystal vault imagined by the ancients. It proves that one even hesitates with regard to the nearest regions; we can scarcely argue about things that are further away. I admit very readily, since the world and the series of numbers are unlimited, an interstellar space in which the billionth or our degrees above or below might be considered as zero.

"Let us never be too affirmative in matters concerning appearances, for they are of little importance. But in placing yourself at the viewpoint of what appears to be the most real, you ask whether the substance of things, such as it appears in phenomena, can be modified. Let us say first of all that the distinction between what is and what appears is only verbal, as it seems to me that I have just proved to you. The veritable creation is that which is manifest. To metamorphose lead into gold, or to cause us to take lead, remaining as such, for gold, is exactly the same work. If the mage gives us the illusion, without anything being different in itself, he acts on our thought. It is a magic greater than that of transmutations, and the true miracle of Cana.

"But we will be in accord with our principles, especially with the most essential one—I mean that of the unity of matter and force—if we admit something more. Perhaps water can be changed into wine in an absolute manner and not only for the eyes and taste of the witnesses. That is to say, since everything is only appearances, could the superior man make that water into wine henceforth, not only for the people who are presently under the empire of his will but also for those outside of his presence, no matter where, who will subsequently be in the presence of that water? When a sage familiar with cases of levitation appears to us to rise from the ground and remain suspended in mid-air, is he affecting our eyes to make us believe it, or does he really rise up? You will grant that the same magic power is manifest in either case, but it is still necessary to respond. He really rises up. The water in the cup is really changed into wine. The appearances can be definitively overturned, not only for an hour and for a limited circle.

"You ought not, however, to admit such contradictions with apparent laws without a serious control. Childishness is to be redoubted and legends are numerous. When Philostratus recounts the story of Apollonius finding himself with his disciples in a plain, the ground of which rose up to give them comfortable seats, I do not see any necessity to believe that naïve assertion. Consider equally suspect any adventure of which you suspect the good faith. I have always had in my principles not to accord any value to experiments made, for instance, by people who are paid. They engage themselves, for money, to show you tricks. Fraud costs them little, in order to produce them at whatever cost, since they have promised them to you. The person who possesses the gift of miracles is not lavish with that sacred gift.

"All power must be discreet. You will recall that Christ refused to manifest his force when he was solicited, before Annas or Caiaphas. From the moment you consent to distract idlers, you are amusing yourself with uninteresting things. You lose your dignity. In addition, you are squandering an energy of which you will sense the loss. Would you go in search of the priestess of Delphi or Cumae to ask her to perform conjuring tricks in a drawing room? They could not come without descending from their pedestal. But the rarity of strange facts, far from being a cause of doubt, is a motive for believing in them.

"Privileged humans have within them the confident will and supreme master that permits them to command material forces and the elements. Faith moves mountains because faith is of another order. It would not be necessary for me to believe in the divinity of Jesus to be persuaded that he walked on water. If you have faith, you will walk. Launch yourself from the top of your house with the absolute conviction that you will descend to the ground slowly without breaking anything. I dare not affirm it, but I am inclined to conjecture that you will not come to any harm.

"The difficulty—I am talking seriously—lies in having that conviction. Saint Peter, going to join Christ on the waters of the Sea of Galilee, nearly drowned half way. That is because he doubted his will. And did not the enemy of the apostle, the magician Simon, also succeed in rising into the air? Were the prayers of the disciple, which caused him to fall and be crushed against the ground by his fall, anything but the expression of a more powerful will, which vanquished him? For here, as in the tales of the Arabian Nights, every magician must fear the formulae of one more powerful. One therefore ought not to disarm oneself as a game and inappropriately.

"Suppose, if you wish, a condensation of being, a fluid created by our internal effort, the influence of which is projected into the exterior world. We do not manifest it externally with impunity. The sage must be miserly with that mysterious gold, for it is a wealth slower to accumulate than to disperse. What is important is not to produce a magical effect at a given moment, but to possess the power."

"All these ideas," said Jean Derève, "appear to me to be accessible, not only to the elite of thinkers, but to the crowd. They come back to a few simple formulae. Could one not vulgarize them, present them straightforwardly, and make magic, in order to employ a clearer expression, a form of religion?"

"That would be a great pity," said Lucia.

Saint-Maur made a gesture of acquiescence. "For myself, I could not see without difficult the disappearance of the sacred woods, whether the gods adored under their foliage are named Zeus or Buddha, and whether the garlands enlace a marble of naked Aphrodite or an image of the Virgin with the blue mantle. Philosophy and science, in order to obtain popular suffrage, lack the belief in a heaven. And the fault of magic, from the point of view of the inferior remainder, will always be explaining the supernatural as the as-yet-unknown natural. One can only capture humans with images and the egotistical hope of a naïve happiness. Every temporary consciousness wants to be sure of eternity.

"That error, toward which I nevertheless have a certain indulgence when it creates beautiful divine forms, explains to us by means of legends where humans come from and where they are going, and puts into the azure old men with white beards on clouds, equipped with thunderbolts. In vain you will tell them, with all rational philosophers, that the gods, if they exist, are impossible for us to know, since the human being is the most perfect form accessible to our thoughts. We are confined in a world and cannot get out of it except by means of dreams and pure supposition.

"Would a luminous insect imprisoned in a block of transparent amber, if it were still alive, have another vision of the universe than that of a milieu transparent and solid to infinity? The highest theogonies all revert to the story of the lion giving his gods the face of a lion. Thousands of men superior in intelligence continue to accept that puerility serenely. If the triangles of geometry books could talk and assemble in council, all of them—the right-angled, the isosceles and the countless host of scalenes—would quickly conclude, by means of irrefutable formulae, that God, if he exists, is evidently the triangle in itself, and perfect. There would be wars of religion in a such a fantastic world, with the army of curved figures, convinced that God cannot be anything other than the perfect circumference.

"The most prodigious effort to avoid that absurdity, to this day, has been the conception of the human-God, a theory that only poses the question, without resolving it, and in a form that demonstrates its insolubility. Will you tell me, with the dogmatists, that God has revealed himself? But he has revealed himself so many times, under such different forms, albeit always human, that it only proves one thing: the power of our varied imagination. Since we can only see humanity in God, would it not be better to depart from the known and seek the divine in the human? Vain hopes. The child demands his images and weeps in order to see them. Assuredly we ought not to make magic a religion. And I console myself with the poets, priests of lies and beauty, for the discomfiture that philosophers experience at that observation."

"You have pronounced the word beauty," said Mathias Corbus. "Some people could invent a religion with that word alone. I think that the particle of truth that every doctrine contains is in the relationship of its beauty, and the splendor of the image, even dead, that it leaves us after it has disappeared. It is bound to desolate you that none of them, even the most charming, can last and that forms succeed one another indefinitely. But progress is eternal. All appearances that persist are bad. Truth that perpetuates itself is transformed into error. But it is necessary to have believed something to perceive its falsity. Let us know how to immolate our ancient gods on the altar of the new god. The most profound and most apparently real speculations of our philosophers will one day be considered infantile chimeras.

"See how we judge the scientific theories of antiquity. Then again, what we call antiquity is only the boundary, very close to us, to which our memory goes back. How different it would be if we could suspect what human life was like two hundred thousand years ago. The end of the Egyptian civilization arrests our vision. We only have legends regarding its commencement. But that epoch is contemporary. Ten thousand years is an hour for humankind. However, we consider as fables the beliefs of that time. As a nation disappears, its gods also disappear, they die and are transported from the temple to the museum. Will it not be the same for ours? By what absurd privilege would one special epoch, that in which we live, for the sole reason that we live in it, escape death? That victory over death and that immobility would be a kind of death itself.

"It is necessary that everything changes and moves. It is the law and progress. It is necessary that today contradicts yesterday while waiting for tomorrow to be convinced of the error of today. 'Verities,' says Pascal—and it is his most profound saying—'will succeed one another with for and against, according to whether one has more light.' He said that in another sense than the one in which I am interpreting it, but it can be applied in a timely fashion.

"If the progress of which we speak exists, and it is the only thing in which it is necessary to believe with all one's soul, our gods will one day by similar to the idols that savages hollowed out in the trunks of primitive trees. Our representations will become infantile and obsolete. Or, rather, they will symbolize, in future times, an ancient and sad dream, like those we see passing through the eyes of apes. Humans have been animals.

"The remotest civilizations worshiped gods with the heads of bulls or crocodiles. They were idols made in the image of primitive men, the worship of which had persisted. We are scornful of our humble ancestors. It is also lugubrious to think that one day, our descendants will believe that they are another race than us. They will smile at our savage mores, our complex and stupid life, our wars, our administrations and our wickedness. Perhaps they will put those of us who remain in cages, for their amusement. Why were we not born later, in the epochs when humans will be superior to us, and even the humblest among them will appear similar to the gods of today?

"But those future humankinds, for us who will one day be the apes, are the future, and this is us. Everyone stands up on the road, in his intermediary place, to receive the torch from the ancestors and pass it on to the children. We shall not be at the fête, but the great final conflagration will only be ignited because of us. I glimpse on the fabulous horizon a temple of splendors. And, imploring them to know that I have seen them coming, I extend my arms toward peoples to be born in a hundred thousand years."

"Unless," suggested Saint-Maur, "a cataclysm occurs, and humankind comes to an end, like a bubble bursting at the surface of a lake."

"That seems to me to be improbable. In any case, nothing would be lost. Another race of beings would depart to join the dead and continue the march forward. There would only be a delay. How do you know that it has not happened before? In any case, it hardly matters. We are on earth to accomplish a task. When it is done, we can die. Or rather, nothing dies; everything is transformed. Death is a illusion. The voyager fatigued by the day's journey believes that the evening will have no tomorrow; but it is absurd to suppose an activity without a goal. The harmony that is revealed in our brief appearance down here is a proof of the beyond. Every minute of our life makes a part of the hour; every hour is a part of a day; every day is a fragment of our terrestrial existence. And our sojourn down here is itself only part of a whole.

"It is necessary not to fear death. It is necessary not to attach ourselves to our dwelling of flesh. How shall I live, I asked myself once, in the epoch of my ignorance, when I no longer have my dear body, when I can no longer see, touch, respire, or kiss other bodies on the lips? Will I even exist? I hold a flower in my hand and I perceive that my hand, my arm and my lips are no more me than the flower is. There is someone inside who makes all that move. There is a soul in the house. Instead of regretting the body, we shall one day be similar to convalescents confined to their dwelling for too long, who are taking their first steps, voluptuously, in the sunlight.

"It is necessary to march toward that deliverance, with hope, and also without haste, for we have a task to complete before the return is permitted. I do not share the illusions of those who find life bad and would like to suppress it. Life is a joyful thing, because of what it announces. It is for us what the eve of a day of leave is for children. Let us leave the nihilist sects to preach renunciation and voluntary death. Let us not be lured by that chimera, and by the dream of a humankind whose members will disappear successively, in order that the future day might come when only a single will dwell upon the earth, the Adam of the return. That is too simple a concept. We ought to follow our path; for our effort matters, and contributes to the definitive result.

"But there cannot be, and this is already consoling, an absolute departure between what we call life or death. What an error Christianity made in surrounding such a natural act with such lugubrious ceremonies and drapes of mourning! What a contradiction with the very principles of that religion! I find the mores of ancient people far superior, who, without even knowing the meaning of death, and without regarding it as anything other than a sleep, had nevertheless divined that the slumber in question was happy. They wanted perfumes, roses and songs of delight around the body. Or rather, humankind ought to be wise enough to pronounce, at that solemn hour, a judgment on the dead. Those who had accomplished the proof and who had merited departure for a better sphere would be glorified; those who had not been able to profit from their existence in order to progress, and who would doubtless return in similar form, of perhaps fall lower, would be lamented without being criticized.

"For the earth is Hell, or one of the circles of Hell. And I do not want that word to be taken in a figurative sense. It is the veritable Hell of the theologians. It is sufficient, in order to be convinced of that, to look around. Sit down on a boulevard bench and look at the people passing by. How many demonic faces! This one bears in his features the infamy of lust, that one base envy. One thick-lipped mouth parades its gluttony. In sum, it is the anonymous, innumerable herd of those who commit the grave sin a hundred times a day, the sin against the spirit; it is the host of fools, the egotistical, vain and cruel people who do not understand. It gives rise to a great pity to see people passing by.

Have you descended into the dens of vice where the lees of the population gather? It is another circle of Hell, with its male and female demons, and its lugubrious décor. Have you paused, in salons of fake luxury, around gaming tables? Have you contemplated the despair of those tortured by a form of amour? All passions are merely complicated instruments for causing suffering, but the most lamentable of the damned are the amorous. They have no repose or truce. Every charming phantom is for them a future torturer. They seek desperately the sensuality that flees them. At least, if they are lamentable, they are not odious. And if they represent torment and anxiety more frightfully than the others, their anxiety is the mark of their predestination; for Hell is not eternal, and at certain moments, one can even glimpse paradise.

"Hell has for a symbol the Devil, who is separation. The Devil falls from Heaven, draws away and then becomes a god again. All things, originally, repose in the bosom of the divine unity. They are dispersed, and it is that distancing from which we suffer. But there is a rhythm in the universe. It is departure and return. It is not Adam to whom the divine unity has said 'Increase and multiply,' but it is by virtue of a fatal and sad law that it should be thus. We have had a fall, and our soul is lost in the bosom of multiform matter. It is necessary to recover ourselves and reunite ourselves.

"The sages of all times have understood that great problem. The search for the philosopher's stone, which transmutes metals into gold, is nothing but the symbol of that profound verity. See how vivacious that belief is and how it explains the majority of our conventional ideas! At all times humans have worshiped gold; it is in vain that moralists have risen up against a sentiment whose meaning escapes them. If we love gold it is because it represents for us the magical power of transmutation. It is because it is the true magician.

"I read a tale somewhere of which the interpretation is easy, and which shows that prodigies are simpler than is believed. A genius appears to the hero of the tale, a kind of Faust saddened by the problem of life. He gives him a purse full of talismans, which are gold disks on which the heads of man are represented, surrounded by engraved characters. 'All that you can desire,' he says, 'you will have by sending one or other of these talismans as a messenger. I am talking about human things that are found on earth, like precious or charming objects whose possession gives joy. Do you want flowers? Give a talisman. You will only have to wait for the time necessary for it to reach the place where the flowers are. They will be brought to you immediately. Would you like to see the most sumptuous meal spread out before you? Give the purse from which the gold is taken. You will only have to close your eyes to see on the table, when you open them again, the mot flavorsome dishes and the rarest wines, everything that can satisfy your inferior sensuality. Would you like paintings, statues? The work of the genius is for sale. And even if you want amour and it resists your gold pieces, you can easily change that insufficient metal for more imperious talismans, pearls and emeralds, diamonds and rubies.'

"The genius was right. What power is more magical and more astonishing than gold? Gold becomes everything and everything becomes gold. It is a figure of unity. Let us refrain from cursing it, like people who only consider its misdeeds. The transmutation that the philosophers sought has been operating for a long time. How do we know, besides, that in the bosom of the earth, under the influence of cosmic forces, various metals do not metamorphose? And if the symbol of fire unites all symbols, doubtless its image, the terrestrial fire, fuses rare metals together. It is necessary to be a devotee of gold, which is only cooled fire. It is necessary to be a devotee of fire, which is the most visible sign for us of the return to unity. And I believe that the moment has come when those who do not understand these things will have to undergo the greatest evils.

We have ceased to render to the true gods the homage that is their due. They remind us, sometimes in the most terrible and cruel fashion. There can be no other explanation for the cataclysms that come to desolate humankind at intervals. Earthquakes and volcanic eruptions are warnings from the gods. Great conflagrations are manifestations. We live alongside fire. We live on it. It is only just never to forget it. It is not the real god, but it is its image. And what terrible faces that power puts on. It is Moloch or Jehovah, in spite of the efforts of humans to substitute Jesus or Buddha It is the god that it is necessary to appease by sacrifices of blood and holocausts. Woe betide us when we neglect the altar from which the flame rises, when we case to burn victims and incense. The god growls and its anger annihilates nations.

"Have not the prophets of all times announced, in any case, that the earth we inhabit must one day perish by fire? An encounter with a heavenly body that is still igneous would be sufficient. Such encounters are not impossible *a priori*. Various worlds undoubtedly gravitate in the immense ether. Has there not been a Deluge, inexplicable by the supposition of the expansion of terrestrial waters? I am inclined to believe that it was caused by the appearance in our vicinity of a particular heavenly body, a planet of water. Why should there not be heavenly bodies composed of a single substance, or rather, elements associated in a certain form. The approach of that liquid sphere, in which the Earth was drowned for a few days, has given birth to traditions that we rediscover in the antiquity of all peoples; and the Earth is humid because of that.

"The creatures that lived down here before the Deluge were different from others not only in form but in nature. A new generation, to which we belong, a humid race, followed the appearance of the water. Why should we not encounter, in future time and space, a planet of fire? It would be the end of the present world. But you know very well that reality is not material, and that I am only speaking here about images. Appearances would vanish in the bosom of the ardent hearth. There is another reunion, and this one is only the symbol. The eternal fire has a superior essence. It allows what is best and durable in us to subsist. No dread can come to us from the sun and volcanoes, provided that we honor them as the face of God. God is the invisible fire, that of the soul, amour.

"And I am coming back, as on a chariot launched in an elegant curve, toward the ideas that we have expressed already. Amour and beauty go together. A religion of amour would be that of beauty. You were right a little while ago. But it is necessary to comprehend amour in the broadest and most fecund sense."

"It would be strange," said Jean Derève, "if, at the end of a philosophical banquet, one did not talk about amour. Plato would have held it against us. On the contrary, I can easily see appearing, in the midst of weary talkers, the young god clad in crimson, with his white wings and his golden quiver. May he always be present, and never accompanied by his brother Anteros, the nocturnal child with the furled wings. I regret that there is no poet in our assembly who could celebrate appropriately the eternal and charming Eros."

The night had almost passed. Through the closed curtains the dubious twilight appeared. The flowers on the table had faded, and the candlelight was paling.

Lucia leaned toward Mathias Corbus. "How," she said, should we mark the devotion that it is necessary to have to the celestial fire that you have revealed? How can we realize the union and the return?"

"By means of the will," said Corbus, "that is the desire of amour and the true interior fire. Let us develop our power. Let us put ourselves in harmony. Magic is only the science of formulae that can aid our effort and summarize it. That effort is within us, and then outside of us. As we obtain more consciousness of ourselves, it will be easier for us to know the universe.

"One emerges from Hell by means of science. Do not listen to the evil devotees who condemn the worshipers of the sacred fire to the pyre. Science is one of the keys to paradise. You can unite the forces scattered around you, but it is necessary to know them. The magic word is not learned in a day. The lyre makes the stones move and builds the walls of the city. It summons around it the charmed lions and tigers, which become similar to lambs. But not everyone who chances to come along can play the lyre. In order to enchain in its wake the elementary genii, it is necessary to have studied the laws that preside over the universe. It is necessary to possess to dominate.

"One emerges from Hell by means of will. There is no durable prison for the person who wants to escape. Science gathers the forces, and the will directs them. After having read all the books and the dusty manuscripts, one finds one day among the hieroglyphs the word *fiat*. The truth is not only knowing but acting. Before even having distinguished the slightest feature of the face of the unknown, let us set forth toward the unknown. All good intentions will encounter one another at the crossroads, before the nocturnal altar of the goddess. But the most welcome will be those who place on the altar the most beautiful sacrificial bouquet to the return.

"That is science and will, which are nothing without amour.

"One emerges from Hell by means of amour. It is the veritable sacred fire. It is necessary to know; it is necessary to want; it is necessary to love: a golden crown, an iron crown, a crown of fire. The will must have its goal outside of us. It is necessary to love everyone. Hatred is the only mortal sin, the sin of fools. It is necessary to welcome all hands, even those that are never held out to us, and to seek lips, all lips, untiringly. One only draws away in order to return. The nation of Hercules is a voyager marching through the immensity toward the primitive nebula. It is necessary to know the multiple in order to discover the unity. The gates of the city are open. The crowd stands timidly on the edge of life; its members scarcely go as far as the nearby meadow to pick a flower before hastening to return.

"It is necessary to go further afield. Differences are bad but necessary. The mirror is other than the face, but it permits it to see itself.

"Others travel a long way and come back laden with trophies. The triumphal gate is opened before them, or, even better, a breach in the wall. Fortunate is the one who, on wings, brings a soul back to the hearth!

"Amour has all forms. It is the only essential thing. Even, and above all, when one is suffering, it is the great initiator. Terrestrial amour accompanies suffering because it is a Heaven in Hell. Amour is the living fire that reunites appearances in order to destroy them, which consumes phantoms in order to form a beautiful bright and rising flame.

"Amour is the gate of Hell, open to the road to Paradise."

POEMS IN PROSE

Sad Pride

For the woman on the sea shore

When I encountered you it was doubtless the same evening when I was to play the divine role of Hamlet; I already had the make-up of the impossible on my face and the flame of imaginary passion in my eyes, and it seems that I did not have the leisure that evening to love you, for an august ceremony was being celebrated in my soul with gold and chasubles, and you know that in the fêtes of the Intellectual, women's smiles are only admitted as candlelight.

That evening, however, was one of fatigued smiles and pale lips, with which I murmured to you what it would have been ungracious of you, Madame, not to take for the most delicate of confessions.

Very impertinently, I kissed your glove, and made the necessary compliment on the flower detached from my spray, which you had put in your hair. And truly, you appeared so charming and so rare that evening that in the music of the orchestra I believed that I recognized the voice of Ophelia, and I told you how much I loved it.

You loved me after that, you too; but beware: for loving art or the artist many have already died, and almost all the others have gone mad. Listen, this is what happens to those who ought never to love art.

Our amours have changed country and moon; we are the adorable adolescents of liturgical music and the servants of Eternal sensuality; but our voices die on our lips before we have disappeared, and we pass through real things as a troupe of actors and lovers that the old king of Bohemia is sending for his pleasure to his cousin the king of Thule passes through the picturesque streets of little towns, making the nocturnal pavement ring.

Counsel

As I fell asleep over some volume of vain science or dolorous beauty, the sun, which was languidly tinting all my thoughts yellow, disappeared. Then the daylight succumbed, with a desperate appeal that I can still hear. Night fell over the roads and the red windows in the walls of the lost château.

But in vain I tried to abandon myself to the land-scapes that are born in the soul, the last of which is incessantly one of the most heart-rending novelty; all the clouds had folded up.

She came in, as usual.

"It's unnecessary," she said to me, "to dwell in obscurity. I've come and I've brought the lamps. Your eyelids are heavy from having been reading." She had become emotional while climbing the stairs. Serious, she sat down, a cherished anxiety in her voice, and became sad over the yellow books with slightly worn black titles.

"You've locked yourself away with books for a long time, and poets who, being dead, are luminous demons, their temples circled by the leaves of the blackest cypress. It's necessary not to love the dead before the hour when we die. Read verses, turning the pages of the thin volumes of times past; they are light tombs that you carry in our hands, If you wanted, if you wished, all the windows would be closed; the books in the depths of cupboards would tell your their magical stories. We would abandon the cities of the world and the rivers bordered by ramparts—oh, the beautiful river!—we would have more cheerful hearts; our shoulders would be curbed under hope as under a cherished burden. I know the key to all this: the only thing is to live. You have surely never loved."

I gazed at her and I had confidence, but she remained silent and her eyes inclined toward me. Soon her irises were no more than distant blue clearings. In the trees, their hands linked, young women were singing in a supple circle.

The Ladies of Heart
A Pantomime

The inevitable Pierrot. The Ladies of Heart. An Englishman. The Case of the Equality of Triangles. A Piano-Mistress. Conventional Formulae. The Only Beloved.

The Ladies of Heart arrive on the stage, where Pierrot is already present; they are of all the colors comprised between pale pink and dark brown. Their hair is curled at discretion, and of varied shades, for the different amorous follies; the young women in question form the antique chorus. Their evolutions are illuminated by a glow coming from the hall, about which more will be said in due course. They begin by striking poses, modest, lascivious and others. In a corner, Pierrot watches. A piano-mistress arrives, who puts her scroll of music on a stool and in front of the young women, without apparent effort, starts leafing through an album of drawings originating from Belgium. They must be very obscene, because there is none of them who does not blush. The others continue to strike poses; then they go away. Pierrot remains alone.

An Englishman in the hall, exasperated by French affectations, makes a few allusions in bad taste to the Russian alliance. An indignant protest rises on all sides. The members of the audience put on their top hats, to which they have attached little black and yellow flags, with the most disgraceful effect. Everyone applauds.

The orchestra saves the tsar once again.

The Englishman does not consider himself beaten. He requests a role in the play. At the third of two he knocks on the door to the wings. Pierrot takes a muted lantern and goes to open it. The Englishman enters dressed as a clergyman. Behind him are the ladies of the corps de ballet, transformed into rigid young English-women. The Englishman salutes Pierrot and makes the introductions.

"My daughters."

"Oh!" says Pierrot.

He thinks momentarily about asking for news of milady, but prudently changes is mind, thinking that the Englishman might be married under the morganatic re-gime.

The claque gives an ovation to the young misses.

The first one is named Jo and the second is named Lo. Those young women, as we shall see shortly, have read Catulle Mendès.[19]

Everyone is very weary. The Englishman asks for rooms. Beds are brought on to the stage. The father claps his hands. "The prayer!" he says.

The adorable young misses open heavy eyelids and rosy lips. A very pretty girl chants a psalm. The others respond.

The father claps his hands again. "Gymnastics!"

---

[19] The flirtatiously loquacious Jo and Lo are two stock charac-ters employed by Catulle Mendès in the many vignettes of contemporary Parisian life that he contributed to newspaper in the late 1880s and 1890s.

He explains to Pierrot that his daughters have the habit of doing a few exercises of flexibility every evening, for the sake of hygiene.

Pierrot does not raise any objection and puts in his monocle.

Then, each adorable little miss takes off her hat, her mantle and her dress. They stand there for a moment in corsets and white bloomers, a little tight on the rosy flesh, with black stockings. Soon, having obligingly undressed one another, with stray hands and frissons of alarm, they appear stark naked, my dear, and lie down on the beds.

The exercises commence; they lift their arms and bend their legs in cadence. The smallest have troubling gaucheries. The big sisters come to the aid of the darlings with their rosy fingers. They lean over, straighten up again, arch their backs, crouch down, and lift up their little warm and firm breasts. Pierrot finds all that very interesting.

Finally, at a signal from the clergyman, they put on their fine chemises again, which cling to secret places, their skin moistened by a perfumed sweat.

Pierrot, naturally, is dying of amour.

He is sent out for a minute, for the young women want to put on their nightcaps; it would not be appropriate for a man to be there.

Then everyone goes to sleep, and the curtain falls...on slumber.

The principal character in the drama is very embarrassed. He is in love with all the young misses and does not know in what terms he should address his declaration to them. He walks around the stage, all alone, and melancholy. Then the Conventional Formulae present themselves. Some of them are dressed as notaries, others as opera tenors. Conversations begin, in a very bored tone.

"How are you, my dear?"

"I'm wearing my mother's cross."[20]

"It's raining."

"Fine weather we're having."

"The winter will be colder than usual."

After that exchange of polite remarks, everyone whispers in one another's ear, and the Case of the Equality of Triangles arrives. That character has an isosceles triangle for a body and invites everyone to feel his angles as others offer their muscles, conceitedly. After having disgusted the audience with his pedantry, he walks back and forth at the front of the stage with a majestic stride, repeating excitedly: "I'm a living theorem, I'm a living theorem." Pierrot would like to ask him for a formula of declaration, but he is intimidated.

Meanwhile at the back of the theater, some monsieur is pleasing everyone and cannot please himself. Two parasites affirm that a reheated dinner is never any good, and nearby, Voltaire, summoned by an old aunt who has fallen ill in the provinces, is packing his trunks; with all sorts of precautions he wraps up his hideous smile in order to preserve it from railway accidents.

Pierrot regrets having read Musset. The spectators, to judge by their sniggers, suspect him of having obtained a few small favors during the entr'acte, but he

---

[20] "His mother's cross" is a phrase coined by Paul Féval to refer to a standard device of theatrical melodrama, by which a long-lost child is finally recognized by some token given to him in infancy.

does not seem any happier for it. He sings a few ballads, but no one listens or arrives. The leader of the orchestra taps his lectern and distributes books of musical scores. The orchestra plays pastorals, and then, gradually, a Swiss milking song. Then the young women arrive, disguised as Unterwalden cows. Pierrot hastens forward and speaks to them in Hebrew. They respond by lowing: "Moo! Moo!" Pierrot understands that they will never again make any other response to his amorous fantasies. The public applauds furiously. That costume is definitely the one that they like best.

Meanwhile, alongside the stage, in a balcony box, a young woman is sitting, with adorable gestures and ironies in the depths of her eyes, who is the only one who comprehends Pierrot's melancholy phrases. Watching with a noble and very disdainful air the drama in which he is the eternal victim of mockery, she smiles strangely, and her smile illuminates the stage and the characters like a torch; and, distractedly leaning over the velvet of the box, she tries on masks of all colors one after another, in order to amuse herself.

Letter to Manon

It's necessary that I tell you, Madame, what happened to me the other day. As I was going along the street, a carriage of old-fashioned form came along, jolting over the cobblestones. The horse puling that carriage was truly apocalyptic, and such a sad figure that it was fearful to look at, and I would certainly have given it a sou had I not reflected that the money would be perfectly useless to it.

That horse had mortuary eyes, eyes that seemed to be composed of all lugubrious things, the pale yellow of mourning candles, with more than one black tear in the middle, wept by an iris, and the horse itself had the gait of a catafalque breaking a church ban, a catafalque of crazy ideas

That horse was pulling a carriage, my dear, since it's to amuse you that I'm writing these rather cheerful things. And this is where the adventure seems to escape from an illustrates tale of fays; that carriage was the most delightful old carriage of which one can dream, a little dog-eared, as if it had been displayed on a shelf for a long time; it had black rods outside and golden rods inside to limit all the regular planes of the carriage, which the horse, as I've said, was drawing over the cobblestones with jolts.

The springs of the vehicle were groaning for the times of Louis XV and the Regency, which they had known, and one wondered what charming face was about to light up in the profound bay; but perhaps the carriage is empty, and it is a long time since hands have been lifted up in order to assist the beloved to descend when she comes back from her long voyage, taller and prouder than when she departed, with I know not what enthusiasm in her eyes.

The interior is hung with golden wands and old, very pale silks, with a provision of furbelows to repose the arm or to incline the head, and drawers hidden in the fabric to contain all the amusing or delicate things that are necessary. The old silks, worn and bright, represent the usual Watteau landscape, melancholy balusters in the depths of a blue forest, on which the women that the carriage carries will surely never lean. But one has the impression of traveling within a narrow horizon, which the trees outside can complete through the window; that gives the adventure something reminiscent of a departure of Bohemians, carrying with them their heart of sunlight.

You were once sitting in the landscape, Madame, and your hair, in a delicate arch, descended over your forehead following a line of beauty, while I gazed at your child-like eyes and I took your slender hands; but you left me your eyes, and withdrew your hands, with a gesture that I followed all the way to the highest treetops of the park.

It was on a fragile and calm evening; large trees were close by, and pools the color of silky dead leaves, into which we would have looked down, if we had not been afraid of seeing ourselves in the night.

It was on a fragile and calm night that the gilded door of my soul opened, where the crazy comedy of the external world was being played, with violins and closed shutters, as if in a Trianon of dreams, and my memories were borne away in the carriage hung with Watteaus, through an unknown city, all black with charcoal and wood, where men clad in black frock-cats that swept all the ways down to the heels were hastening at the street corners, with monotonous speeches, among the carriage, under the damp gray sky.

But the landscape that I was carrying, the silky trees of fabric and the grace of women sitting at the cross-roads of the forest, all those things were the frame in which I want to travel, alone with my thoughts—quite alone, you understand—with the person whose gestures are for me the unique pretext of a horizon. I have no need, I think, to name you.

Moonlight

On the terrace paved with jade, like a dream more diaphanous than the gray wings of bats, the little princess advances fearfully under the pale rays of moonlight.

The moon marches, saddened, through the rapid clouds, illuminating the roofs of pensive pagodas and rendering the shadows of bushes sharper.

Along the terrace paved with jade, at the foot of which dragons with chimerical forms are asleep, the little princess advances, her silk dress rustling furtively.

Oh, in what path of dreams is she thinking of posing her delicate feet? What can her dark eyes, so strangely alarmed by kohl, distinguish in the obscurity?

Does she have exotic dreams of an unhealthy incoherence, the kind that come to us when we sense in the depths of the soul in all its intensity the evil of living? Is the musical charm of her gaze born of the bizarre sadness of her thoughts?

Above the bushes full of shadows, amid the frail and fine latticework of black branches and white flowers, the roofs of pagodas glisten.

Is she evoking, nostalgically, the distant landscapes of old Europe, where scenes of unknown amours sketched under plane trees on the edge of great lakes?

It is a summer night, calm and scintillating. The profile of the princess is silhouetted delicately on the moonlit walls. A svelte golden butterfly, immortality, rises from her hair, and beneath her eyelids, irises full of an indecisive velvet have the charm of the night.

The water of pools into which black leaves are falling shines and plunges to infinity, and the memory of ancient things settles like a perfume on the calices of flowers, opening slightly to respire the shadow.

And, her soul full of the night and the vision of the impossible, with a silky rustle of her painted dress, the princess sits down on the jade steps, and, without knowing why, begins to weep.

Saddened, the moon marches through the rapid clouds.

Watercolor

The table is black lacquer, the curtains yellow and black; the sunlight of the windows makes gems of a thousand colors float in the room; the thought of the beloved is reflected and multiplied in the same way when she gazes into my obscurely illuminated soul.

On the black lacquer table, which is covered by a worn gold cloth, emerald-colored glasses put a new and esthetic joy into their radiance tined with forgetfulness.

In the emerald-colored glasses a few rare flowers are placed, not for the brutal and confused harmony of a bouquet, but for the unique outlines of each, and their perfumes: a mimosa and a chrysanthemum, solitary and delicate, are subtly sculpted into works of art.

Etchings gaze enigmatically from the walls, and fans evocative of polychromatic countries, bizarre roofs and blue mountains, suggest calm reveries, with the hint of exoticism that is sufficient to satisfy the unhealthy desire for novelty.

And thus, in that interior, slowly, with the neat and delicate touch of a patient water-colorist, I amuse myself by designing black letters on Japanese paper, which are made symmetrical by regular and unfinished lines—for the woman by whom I am loved...

For The Astonished

When you wanted to look at me—with your large sad eyes—you said to me; "Dear pessimist, what are you thinking about?"

I smiled, captured by the charm—About that lying April—laughter in the cry of alarm—that warned me of the danger.

A confession, of which the soul—is a wing to flap—to fly away—oh, what gradation!—to go up to the pigeon-loft!

All lips toward your lips—might as well be disturbed... Sèvres porcelains...decorate the light wall.

Wander in my crazy fields—a madman, very sad and very handsome... Your gazes are symbols—and your smile a torch!

He asks for help—will you shelter tomorrow—in the profound and sad refuge—the nocturnal rose in your hand?

That mad thing, with neither queen nor master—when it had, mocking yesterday—sung too much for your window—is singing today for your heart.

Chat

You have often dreamed, don't deny it, of the mysteries of the beyond. That was my fault, a romantic and puerile lover, in the nuptial chamber, in the first evening, an ivory cranium on black cushions.

But for the burning glow of the candles that I had wanted soft and yellow, like those that are deformed at the back of familial cupboards among bundles of fabric and objects of blessed box-wood, could one be sure that at the supreme moment, the incense would not fuse in the room, in order to make your white shoulders shrug in a movement that I could believe to be irony or sensuality. It was the décor. I have learned since that all landscapes are internal. You, better informed, have forgiven me those slight lapses of taste.

But you knew, and those who have known never forget it, what chain of subtle gold links voluptuousness to death, and that that banal image, of waves so often violet, is the only one that has not yet undergone an absolute shipwreck. You have not learned amour in my eyes. I would have sworn, however, that my innate sadness had poured into your heart.

We got up at dawn to read the books and pronounce the usual formulae of the desperate, as one hastens to go further. Our lips no longer experience a frisson, except at the kiss of magic philters. It would be difficult for us to respire a flower. That is not sufficient.

Imagine that a distant city is buried in the sea. The sirens came toward the beach, the eddies of the waves have told me. Little children, on feast days, marched sagely in the streets to the sound of bells. The fabulous memory of galleons laden with gold rose from the sea-bed like a wave. A city is at the bottom of the sea. It reposes under the weight of submarine atmospheres. The bells are reefs. It is astonishing to see them so delicately cut out. The bays will never again be empty of glaucous water, nor will the divine air be respired. They will crumble without being woken from that liquid nightmare. The bronze bells, embroidered with moss, no longer ring. It would be necessary to go out there, into the city at the bottom of the sea.

Where do you want to take your folly? Out of the world, I know that very well. We have traversed countries the very name of which makes travelers go pale. There is the city of fear where, under a sulfurous sky, faces worn by fear have thin lips that chant, and the heads, under mourning hoods, turn round furtively, as if pursued by a misfortune that is about to fall. There is the city of opium, with its porticos draped in red curtains and the passage of Roman consuls. Its high walls rise on the horizon of sand, as white as a luminous slumber. And there are other frightful cities. The facades make gestures with wrought iron gallows. Behind the windows of the upper floors, well-behaved children are sitting, outlining colored images in the transparency of the evening. There are stories and tales. Oh, those too. Hostelries are open and diligences are departing in the distance; the long gray roads are ribbons that the postillion's whip is unrolling like a fuse. Out there, beyond the trees, is the moon again; and then the sea, the supreme goal of efforts.

It is the Sea of Galilee, on a Sunday morning. We are not prophets, to go and meet one another on the sea.

And whether it is as furious as on evenings of tragic downpour, or as calm as a liar, the path over its waves is not reliable. The shore is traced with footprints. Others are already wrapped in their cloaks in order to die there, their eyes closed. They had surpassed all the mages. One can scarcely see the shadow of Apollonius vanishing beyond the cruel rocks. What folly made them build, with the timbers of their ship, the red nocturnal pyre, in order to weave around it the dance of their dead dreams?

No more ships, no more boats: shore that no one will ever attain, let us ornament you in recompense with all the necklaces of magic. We are in love with the impossible and we do not want to be consoled. On an immemorial and fabulous beach, immortally sad and beautiful, the child of my pride and my speech, my superb dream is asleep, on an immemorial and fabulous beach, so distant that the great birds of eternity would weary the flight of her black wings without reaching it.

The Obscure Soul of Golden Caskets

Put to sleep by the room, you gaze at length, as in scenes of opium. The furniture and the fabrics, eternalized by time, respire far from the heart and far from life. Statuettes with durable poses, are you not as real as our fugitive thought? A serene form will sing being, uniquely by its line, ignorant of the frisson. Born from the shadow are the works of art and the beautiful things that no care can wound: they have no soul, or the obscure soul of jewels and gold caskets.

The jewels that your hands caress have been caressed by other hands; they have made the pride of other fragile flesh, have calmed by their bright magic many fevers of heavy brows—and gold caskets, in what distant Italy, cradled by the waves, have they voyaged without you? For sailors sleeping under the stars, the flanks of the ship contain regal melancholies. Handle the tarnished and patient chasubles where the splendor of evenings fades away. I think of the defunct joy that beautiful objects express but do not experience.

She is lying in the midst of strange flowers. Her lips will not part for the usual sobs; the one who is sleeping has bid a weary adieu to walks in the dusk of cities or in the vibrant mornings, with umbrellas and blue dresses. More dead than something that has never lived, a form alone laughs at the mystery—her hair, for a while, has been scattered n the pillow, and her soul is similar now to that of things. It is the obscure soul of jewels, chasubles and golden caskets.

Dream

I spent my days in the shady pathways of a vast promenade planted with trees, where the street-lights shed a tranquil light in the evening.

All around stood tall houses of desolate appearance, similar to those one sees in provincial cities, where thousands of lives go by, sometimes vulgar and full of the materiality of existence, sometimes sad, unreal and darkened by a melancholy anxiety.

Under the great trees through which the sunlight passes, tracing fleeting luminous designs on the ground, I see groups of woman advancing, all resembling something once dreamed, and darting strange glances at me. They are astonished to see me like this, motionless, careless of the rapid flight and the leaves swirling in the air and coming to land at my feet.

On seeing those women pass by, bizarre thoughts and bewildered visions come to me. Those of all times appear to me; the Queen of Sheba, Cleopatra, Sappho and Lilith, the first woman, that of sin, appeared to me in the window of an antique manor, full of the sadness of times past.

However, I could not help thinking about the little flower-seller that I once saw, I forget where, with blue eyes and little blue veins on the temples, whose laughter bit my heart.

But when the time came, the apparitions disappeared and I heard a distant music that moved me profoundly, and I thought I was hearing the music of Weber.

And then I had the confused sensation that all those things had happened a long time ago, that many dear lives were extinct, and that there would no longer be anything but silence and desolation, where so many humans had lived.

Meanwhile, years went by slowly; the grass grew around me. Soon it rose higher than the trunks of the old trees, higher than the old tall houses in the windows of which the reflection of distant fêtes remained in which I had once danced.

There was no longer anything but a vast forest, full of murmurs, swarms of insects and sunlight. But I remained motionless, not daring to venture through the shady pathways, and dreading, if the wind agitated the branches, that I might feel sheaves of memories being shed over my head.

The Mistresses of Poets

The mistresses of poets are thin; they are the women with the bodies of children who, at dawn, while the beloved sleeps the heavy slumber of the ending night, get up in the crepuscular gleam. They go through the narrow bedroom, lighting the fire, disposing the white sheets that ought to collect the thought of the poet, and the dear books, too often read, that haunt his insomnias They are cold, in spite of the lighted fire, being among those who dream anxiously of being buried in the soft warmth of the bed and sleeping, sleeping forever, caressant and caressed, with black hair, a pensive forehead and lips quivering with the fearful ignorance of everything that is not the kiss. And in the morning, soon risen, vigilant, but with heavy eyes, they come to lean over, bewildered, the closed eyes of the lover, like the black velvet page in the old German legends who watches over the white lovesick page.

The mistresses of poets are ugly, but their ugliness is full of a charm to make one weep. Their eyes have a mystery and their lips the divine smile that humiliates beauty. And for the one that vulgar desires would scorn, the poet feels the source of his wounded heart opening; and the eternal song, as on the fragile strings of a sonorous violin, weeps its vibrant harmony in their desolate soul. O seductive and melancholy beloveds, what subtle and sad demon informs them of the dear secret of curing the disease of living by means of the disease of loving? Alas, it is of a disease that others might perhaps find strange that the poet is dying today, O sister of yore and poor pale child whose heart was so frail, her long black hair so caressant, and the frisson of whose eyes was unforgettable for such a long time.

The mistresses of poets are dead. During their terrestrial life, so brief, they were called Lilith, Antigone, Sperata—and it is them, who died of amour, whose kiss we seek on the lips of today. Oh, how eternal the wound is—to be unable to cure hat starry, futile and vain desire—and so dear!—Come the evening, which calms and lulls sick hearts, as one rocks unwise children who see frightening form in the night—And you put the soul of the poet to sleep with ethers and narcotics, so that he reposes in dreamless slumber where all dolor is annihilated. But before that somber dawn descends, he will go out under the moon, toward the tombs where the closed lips are and the eyes forever closed. And when he has confided to the magical quivering silence of the evening the secret of dear words, and luminous poems that no one but him will ever read, they will come, those of old, who alone will have listened; they will come, with caresses and their hair undone to murmur the amorous responses that he had never heard, and yet he recognized.

Prose for the Bacchante

Scene I

The virgins have got up, by night, and have come with a light step into the corridor to see their husbands pass by.

The latter appear. They are weighed down by a fatigue and an immense dolor.

Bitter dolor.
My dear, dear...

(The accompaniment of violins I hear in the distance.)

Remember that those young men have represented Amour since the dawn of the world. According to the calculations of Moses, the most authorized, that makes six thousand years of enthusiasm, slightly worn out today,

The violin is sad and personal. The virgins so not listen to it, for fear of weeping. Their little chemises fold poorly over their naked breasts. Their skin smells good. They have the desirable timidity in the already-comfortable curves of their slender bodies and eternal violets in their eyes.

Scene II
(*The same, the Pipe of Peace*)

(The appearance of that character is welcomed by the sympathetic groans of the audience, which immediately falls asleep.)

The poets arrive, clad in long black robes and preceded by the crucified image of Beauty.

(Perhaps that role is played by one of the virgins, who has not found a husband. She will die of the mystery that she carries within her. The poets do not understand anything, any more than she does.)

The voice of Ollendorff[21] in the wings: "Enter the Editors."

The poets utter groans: "Brothers, it's necessary to die!"

But still the unique violins:

Ha ha! Life!
Ha ha! Death!

The Pipe of Peace, taking advantage of the general emotion, goes to have a drink in the neighborhood. The poets, thinking about Posterity, get drunk on books. The editors have gone.

"That young woman looks too sad don't you think?"

(As one who does not know that noises have been heard in the wall): "Yes, the country air will do her good."

---

[21] Presumably the publisher Paul Ollendorff (1851-1920).

"I'm doomed," she said to me. "I waited for you for too long in the wood. Beware of catching a chill; are you even wearing flannel?"

"Oh," I replied, "the woods are so unsafe by night, and it's so far from your horses!"

"Isn't it?" she said, mocking. (I sensed the dolor in her laughter.)

(Then, always that tune pursuing us.)

The violins were exasperating in the distance, with short pauses. Their voice closely resembles that of bells. They have departed for the stars, where, no doubt, they will find it better to live than here.

The play is finished, the curtain falls. The crowd retires slowly.

"Monsieur!"

"Yes, Monsieur! You say...someone has squashed your hat in a box. That doesn't concern me. I'm not a hatter. I'm the theater manager. Besides which, we're very busy...unfortunate incidents...

"The young woman who was playing the role of Beauty has just died. She begged me to ask you to excuse her."

Eulogy

Scilicet eximius Tibicen Antonius.[22]

The old women who are spinning and telling tales are sitting by the fireside under the mantel of the high fireplace; what story are they reciting, with their soft lips and overlapping teeth? That of the princess who slept for a hundred years. It is a puerile country. All things knew that they ought to be legendary and conform to that expectation. Pages snore on marble staircases and no footsteps fall. The tapestries in the halls, even the tapestries, reproduce stories of slumber. But here comes the dawn; someone is knocking at the exterior door; it is the king's son. The advent seems impossible; they have been asleep for such a long time. He has traversed the forest, cutting down the trees. The lady smiles and wakes up. She gives him her hand, with the same gesture as the ladies of the previous century, in the depths of park, on the edge of divine pools.

The princess who has woken up is the glory of Watteau. Doubtless, for a long time, poets have celebrated him, who wears in white, as one does in China, the

---

[22] Namely, the excellent piper Antonius. The painter Jean-Antoine Watteau (1684-1721)—the inventor of "fêtes galantes" and the painter of the famous "Pilgrimage to Cythera" or "Embarkation for Cythera," echoed in the title of one of Charles Baudelaire's most famous poems—was more usually known as Antoine Watteau.

mourning of his heart. But today, people talk about a marble bust in the same Luxembourg where he once came to copy the effects of light in the trees—men and women with lorgnettes who have come in pilgrimage, their arms rounded, their expressions impertinent, with the entire cortege at the water's edge. A mask laughs, depositing a wreath of pink and black roses on the marble in the form of an altar. He knows that glory is not worth a fly assassinated at the corner of the mouth,[23] to the left side, that of the heart. But since posterity wishes it! Let us eternalize the *fêtes galantes*, let us sing antique hymns, let us summon from the depths of the park, skirts crumpled, red mantles in the wind, the heroes of that Italian comedy, life, in order to render homage to the man who evoked them

Their soul is Watteau; it is a futile and charming soul, scarcely more vibrant, but also more delicately moved, than that of the trees and the evening. The characters in silk mantles, marching silently in the dusk, have come from strange countries where the heart is appeased and attenuated; a sentiment brushes them and passes by, but that sentiment is exquisite, sadness does not last any longer than joy. Watteau remembers his youth, and the apprenticeship he made, in painting white and gilded ceilings. Legend enables his studio to be seen much later; the brushes are scarcely clean. The palette is overloaded with colors of every sort, the tones mingle, the deep layers are a somber and sad amalgam, and the painter, with his brush, skims delicately; he takes the flower and the down of his palette, without ever attain-

---

[23] The French term for an artificial beauty-spot was *mouche* [fly], because of an imagined resemblance to a dead fly.

ing powerful passion and vigorous expression; it is prim, but it is the primness of Watteau.

It is necessary to accept those characters, even unreal. Every painter has a different vision, and each one represents life as he can. This one is a literary painter, the worst species for some. They would like something other than trees, conversations and embarkations, but Watteau's trees, even their imaginary color, are as true as Dutch interiors. He has made use of the worn-out theme of all bad poets and decorators. The white pierrot has suffered abominable outrages and everyone came to write a sonnet in black ink on his pale garment. Such a painter, it seems, is not longer saddened by these homages of carters, and he is known even so in the paths where, amid promenades, his name on the lips was, for other lips, the most delicate of compliments, and also the most melancholy, for the embarkation is toward joy as well as toward a prompt regret. The landscape toward which one is rowing will not open so soon; it closes a very near horizon; the trees surround it completely, and in his passage toward the unknown, the boat, as soon as it has departed, will not weary of landing. Watteau will be loved, without any other reason, for having symbolized, in his boscage, where characters are chatting while waiting sadly—one does not know why—in red heels and sullen dresses, the futile and charming desire for the unknown, and the brief duration of joy.

It is necessary to imagine painters as players of instruments. Michelangelo plated the sublime *de profundis* on the organ. Others, those whose paintings have distances, blue mountains with picturesque ruins, assemble woodwinds shiny with wax-polish; their cheeks inflated by piping are those of shepherd whistlers. By means of shady pasturage and lush grass they declare the calm of the countryside and treetops swayed by a fresh breeze. Here are the violins and the Dutch fêtes, the tankards of beer, the heavy joy of dancing and feet tapping to the rhythm of celebrations. The faces have plump cheeks and shiny gleams on their plane surfaces. Saint Cecilia, her eyes upraised to Heaven, is playing the cithara. The collar of her dress is well designed to frame her virginal neck, and her invisible hair makes her head tilt; the landscape is unreal, as is appropriate. Others, with their brushes for plectra, enable the full spectrum of colors to resonate on painted canvas or wooden panels.

Watteau is the flute-player in the somber green location. The flute voices, in light and mocking fashion, the sorrows of someone who does not believe it. The décor is the same: the motionless trees that form the background will never sway; one sees their fleeting crowns reflected, inverted, in the clarity of the waters, in the fatherland of chimerical clouds that run underground and disappear at some shore of grass; the poplars are rounded in clearings for a conversation, in order that the habitual troupe clad in frivolous silks can come and sit down. "Listen, they're talking over there." It is so little that the talkers are part of the landscape, like the leaves, the mysterious mossy trunks, the balusters and the old fauns that are distinguishable in the depths of pathways with their weary smiles.

Meanwhile, the flute plays; it voices, invisibly, the tremulous joy of loving, the confessions, the confidences, the twilights; and the wandering melancholy that its frail notes recall in a fashion so surprising in the evening—and then, as if ashamed of being languid, it departs in vibrant and aerial notes, and mocks, and plays, stringing out bursts of laughter as if they were sobs. Dusk falls; the noble lords in short cloaks and the ladies with smiling fans go silently into the forest. They go toward the windows of folly, which, the sun having disappeared, are lighting up in the distance, doubtless in order that the fête can continue, in the land of verdure and tapestries on the walls, scarcely more unreal than the real one, with candlelight too; behind them, like furtive footfalls, the flute plays its final notes: sobs or laughter, but very faint. Even the shadow can no longer be distinguished; perhaps it is that if the faun of a little while ago, amusing himself by sowing fear in the boscage.

It is thus that the fantasy speaks. The fête is one of the most futile and most beautiful that one can imagine. If the faces do not have on their lips the enigmatic and divine smiles that make one weep, the gestures of the hands and the bearing of the heads are so noble that one almost forgets, and almost no longer regrets. The décor is always such that one would like to live there, frivolous as the life was. Something trivial gives that joy. From the flute-player, rediscovered everywhere, the most fleeting drawing as well as the most patient canvases reveal the impertinent brush. His sanguine touches would be enough: the design of a mantle over the shoulders, an oblique profile, leaving the eyes the leisure to imagine complete scenes. The fleeting form of a woman who sees beauty passing, gives us a sign that she remembers it. As they are a simple sketch, those red lines leave us more to dream, and more dream has remained in the soul of the man who drew them.

Royal Hands

One king leaned over the cradle, his beard majestic and his eyes very soft. Now he draws away, insouciant, in his beautiful court cloak. But O, the golden vase full of gleaming stones, forgotten before the couch of old wood polished by time! Could the child not pay for a kingdom in fabulous India with that gold?

The second old man has the lamentable face of those who once wept. Cassolettes, as he enters, spread their clouds toward the beams and the chilly spiders. That was incense. Men follow who are carrying more incense in sandalwood caskets, in large grains of gray powder. That was the temple after the palace. The rare caskets, lined with faded old velvet, are laid on the straw. With that incense one could have perfumed all the newborn's future hours like a corolla.

And the myrrh is the tomb. The weary hands of the last king were trembling from his long voyage in the twilight, the stars would have been jealous of the sad beauty of his present. A nocturnal cry had saluted him on his departure, from the height of native cities. This was the king who carried the myrrh with which the dead are embalmed; this was the child who was to open to the dead embalmed with myrrh the door in the depths of the tomb.

For a Demon

Are you now on the eve of disappearing before the phantom of naked life, you whose smile was the beacon of my yesteryear? Will the simple sensuousness of her hands of flame close her eyes habituated to mysteries? Shall I never see you again? Will you, the accursed whose ungraspable presence immortalized my anxieties, put on your face the color of my soul the new magical mask of being, in addition, the disappeared? I would like my prayers to be pagan, in order to praise you as much as I wish. The herald who came to search for us at birth, to summon us to play the role, wore a bracelet of black diamonds.

Your face was supple wind, and my words undulated toward you like the flame of a royal pyre. Your wings shadowed the morning twilight in which my violet sadness recognized itself, in the parks where, out there, above the haughty crowns of the trees, the dead gleams of the sunset came like the sound of horns. On the bosom of young men, in a beautiful tale of antiquity, a sculpted golden cicada sleeps, cradled by an amber necklace. A day arrives when it wakes up, listening to their heart beating.

I know full well that I will die of your amour, one day or another, and that you will hold it against me. But, all decked in lace you strut, letting your languors flow from your long hands like waves of pearly opals, and your brothers in exile come in your wake in a great cortege, with torches, gaze at me with their profound eyes.

The poems they would recite if their lips were not sealed by the distant breath of seas would cause the old priors who, having risen at dawn, lean their foreheads worn by the light of cold cloisters over yellow missals, to pale with regret.

You are as beautiful as a sin, and your gaze is troubled, like eyes in which the divine spasm is plating. No one would weary of seeing you pass by. The supple grace of your body is a hymn to light gods. Sleeping in the hollow of your hand, all gestures disappear. You are also sadness. All other sensualities would wear the robe of censer-bearers before your young sensuality. If anyone named them, it would be a stray syllable of your name.

A memory, which bears your name, after what vanished generations and what furtive apparitions, in usual cities, of young women with beautiful breasts, will brighten the melancholy of adolescents, saddened by their heart in the future, like a dream lantern with colored glass that an unknown page clad in white will come to swing amid the black silhouettes of trees, through the real and lunar parks of their amorous youth.

Wish

At the gates of the city, in the evening—when you pass by among your companions-and the slightly crazy cortege of masks and torches—there is a poor man—whom your gaze renews—and who asks for alms with an augural gesture.

—But you go away—with your sad moue—and the delicate scorn of your curly hair—forgetful—of the hour and the roses—that the black beggar sings under the trees.

—And the cortege—having disappeared at the slight hazard of the shadow—the singer—to console himself—in the music of symbols—has celebrated the death of forgotten springs.

—A hand—digs his tomb—in the same marble that had your form—stark naked—with your sad moue—and the delicate scorn of your curly hair.

For Silla

If I have eaten the tambour and drunk the cymbal, at the hour when I wanted to evoke your memory, it is because I was sure that my intoxication would dilate my eyes in order to see you more clearly. And the poison is only the luminous demon whose wings will cry me to the land of the moon where you were the star danger of some comic opera in shadow and blue.

Now, under my pen, which is designing the quivering forms of your name, the paper becomes a golden leaf, and like the appeal of a magical incantation, the three archangels of amour appear, the seraphim eternally clad in white. Their eyes are dead by virtue of having disdained and their immutable lips remain white, for since the splendid fanfare and the conflagration of the creation, the archangels have only sung three times; the last was to name you, on the eternal day when you were born! I see them and I see their hands opening very wide for me the gates of the lost paradise of madness.

My madness, it is you entirely, and the delicate and vain gaze with which you listened to me, at the time when I told you in a low voice what my heart was singing aloud: "Your flesh is all my horizon, your perfume all my sensuality."

I believe that it is the gift of poets to love once and for all some young woman lost among the wanderers of amour who appear in our universe, for the time to agitate a mask in a chord of a violin, one day when the sun celebrates its most glorious anniversary and the cloisters of great trees forms a vast and quivering cloak for the earth. But the Bohemians of your tribe, in departing for the moon, have forgotten you.

Your eyes, Madame, are Dresden china seen to the sound of music, and your lips are my life. For you alone I have dreamed this frightful and divinely reassuring thing, a pilgrim nestling entirely in the mystery and modesty of your holy grotto, in the most profound of your kisses.

For you return, we all return, both those who weep for beauty and those who are beauty, from some distant and picturesque eternity of which we bear the exile in our eyes. And the poet returns, I imagine, from evening planets where all the forms are immortal and all the paintings luminous; where the sun itself, Madame, is something so vulgar that it would be very difficult to dare, out there, to fashion with the sun an arm-rest of a balcony for young elbows, outside lace and your languor.

The Bust

Talking about him would, too often, be talking about Bohemian things, as if he were not also a pure and distant poet. But he is dead, and as in the glorious renaissance of a soul henceforth alone and without a crazy troop in his wake, what the true Verlaine was will remain, by virtue of the apotheosis of a funeral—the most sumptuous awarded to a poet, popular or great, for a long time. If the child that he wanted to be and who kept the supreme vigil all night on his death-bed, affected, by means of a puerile pout, with his head inclined over his breast, to scold maliciously the one who was coming, more death-like than him, to fetch him, could have had knowledge when morning came of the fête that was in preparation for him, I imagine that his heart would have swelled with a charming vanity. There were more flowers on the bed of mourning than he had received during his entire life. And poets, among whom many were moved and sincere, waited at the threshold to accompany him.

Oh, the pomp of the church, astonished to receive him thus—him, the ingenuous sinner who, at the dawn of ancient days, went to strike the doors of the parish with a reckless staff, requesting confession! Now the organs resonate. And the ceremonial usher advances. Snobbish men, funereal chants, the aspersion of lustral water, the office unfurls like the train of a black velvet cloak. And up above, at the summit of the organ, an upright angel, by virtue of a singular play of light on the pleats of his garment, seems, like some Hindu god, to have two right hands; one leans over, rigid and sinister, toward Hell; the other, benevolently, points to Heaven. What pretexts for sonorous phrases and what imposing décor. The silent crowd fills the church. If the mischievous gamin Lelian, who is musing somewhere, were to venture into the aisles, I think that the doorkeeper with a gilded halberd would abuse him somewhat.

Now the funeral cart sets forth, in the bright winter morning. A magical sun shines in the street, pitting a golden dust over the black drapes. The procession is slow. It passes the bridges and the booksellers...how many familiar memories! But suddenly the road is wider and the décor has changed: in the background, against the intense blue sky, is the Opéra. And there is an unforgettable minute. Before us, the black tricorn of the coachman stands out brutally against the gilded blue on high. A cold wind blows over the fête and makes the flowers shiver. The hearse is carrying the poet to the last Opéra Ball: the hazard of these encounters. It passes shops selling lace and fans. The sun is inimitable. It is in a décor of *fêtes galantes*, a Watteau burial.

That is the way I want to see the death of Verlaine, all the bitterness of past days forgotten, and not remembering the nocturnal walks when the poor poet's charming voice, as he went back up his hill toward dawn, was saying, in an effort of his weary legs: "We won't get as far as the Panthéon!" But the Panthéon is a sad place, an academy for the dead. Its bare, cold walls rise up for other poets than him. The Palace of Westminster is strewn with laureate tombs, but the most glorious tomb is that of the divine Shelley; his body was burned beside the sea and his ashes cast to the blue wind.[24] Verlaine ought to repose in effigy, in the broad sunlight, in groves of trees, in order to summon in pilgrimage the lovers of the distant land of which he dreamed.

Today, as in Westminster, we have a poets' corner in the boscage of the Luxembourg; Banville and Mürger will applaud through the foliage on the day when the white marble of the august bust of another immortal looms up. The man who sleeps outside the walls, like a philosopher, in his little house in the fields, would laugh divinely at his statue, crowned in the midst of poets come at dawn to salute him, and congratulate himself for finally being made of marble. The characters that lament in the exquisite dialogue *Les Uns et les Autres*, will be able to shred their hearts with fearful gestures sitting in the shadow of the bust. And the last glimmers of sunlight, disappearing behind the Luxembourg at the hour when only the undersides of the trees are gilded, will fall upon the head of the faun lying in wait as night falls for the melancholy of nymphs scattered in the melancholy of the forest.

---

[24] It was beside a lake, not the sea, that Shelley was buried, and the laureate tombs are in Westminster Abbey, not the Palace of Westminster, but the errors are insignificant.

Hertulie

The poet came from a street, saluted as he passed, with an amicable gesture, by the people standing next to the columns. Some praised his garment and others his genius. But the most handsome ephebe pointed at the poet's hand. A new ring was glittering there.

"Isn't that," said the courtesan Syra, "the price of a night of amour?"

"Oh," said another, "You came first in the flute competition, and the judges have given you that ring."

But he lifted his finger, smiling. It was a circle of gold in the form of an iron collar. One the bezel, very large, they read: *I belong to Hertulie and I am a fugitive slave. Passer-by, bring me back.*[25]

---

[25] The poem might refer to "Hertulie, ou les messages" (tr. as "Hertulie; or, the Messages") a Symbolist short story by Henri de Régnier, first published in *Le Trèfle noir* (1895). The courtesan Syra is features in comedies by Terence and Plautus.

Opportune Song

First of all, Madame, there were your eyes; let's close the window, if you don't mind; we'll be better able to talk. I don't know why we're having such a bleak winter. First of all, Madame, there were your eyes—but so slightly, your eyes: the red lanterns of an omnibus passing on the boulevard.

Then, there was your flesh, but all your flesh; and when my caresses touched you, it seemed to me to sculpt a statue of joy in the malleable gold of your forms. Then, there was your flesh, but so veritably your flesh that all the old men covered their eyes in response.

Then, there was your heart, but so slightly, your heart! Your heart is like a great theater, with music, rouge and candles; and women reciting fine verses with beautiful gestures, soullessly, and lovers are on the balcony, as well as other ladies, all those ladies on the balcony! My melancholy has knotted its mask, and violins are singing a mocking tune; then, there was your heart, but so slightly, your heart.

An Encounter With the Soul of Watteaus

You want me to amuse you, Madame, with my first glimpse of the soul of Watteaus; gladly, my dear.

That day, we were dreaming about a woman, my soul and I. You know her, since it is the one whose memory breaks my heart when I think of you. And I said to her: "In order that you have captured me so entirely, what a magical power you must have! Certainly, I could easily believe that your soul had been exchanged with the very soul of Watteaus, and that it is gazing at me through your eyes."

At this point the soul of Watteaus appears and laments softly that I am making her serve for such annoying comparisons. She does not want to be confounded with a woman like you. In order to console herself, she evokes a habitual landscape: marbles, verdure, colonnades. In that frame, a cortege arrives of ladies with exquisite smiles and lords with very high heels. They chat, with a thousand charming affectations, and then quarrel in a vulgar manner. The ladies mutter things behind their fans; the lords throw their red shoes at one another's heads.

The soul of Watteaus laments. I slap her to make her shut up. She sobs. I've crumpled her collaret. How, then, can she go to the ball this evening? Then I allow myself to be softened. She's a good little soul, whom I kiss on the eyes. We both set forth, with great foolish gestures, through the picturesque night, and we stop at a Regency café, on the terrace. The waiter serves us stars on a burnished silver tray. Then I take a little violin from my pocket and I make the soul of Watteaus dance.

But why this madrigal to you, Madame, who have no soul and yet resemble so marvelously in body those Watteau souls who have none?

Is it not necessary to burn incense to the women among whom one encounters, you first, and two or three others, and then one I know?

I so often have difficulties with the moon because of you!

You're so naïve, my dear, that it will always remain closed to you.

Your ignorance is, in any case, only the golden clasp of an adorable missal of amour, and, stupid as you are, and so charming, I no longer experience any but a sad joy at your joy. All the preceding is perhaps no more than an ingenious allegory. I know in what eyes the landscapes are evoked in which I want to live, and I believe that if the soul of Watteaus looked at herself in the sculpted mirror of her belt, it is your face that she would see.

The Gift of the Book

I am bringing the aromatics to embalm your house; the bearers have come from afar in nocturnal stages. They are more numerous than the clouds, the perfumes are newer than the wind. You will be proud, I know, of having respired their flower, and you will faint in my arms. No one will ever see henceforth, on future thresholds, as many aromatics as I have given you for your house.

I shall give you sandalwood to enclose your house, that perfumed house. With that light wood I shall make balustrades for your divine arms, and harps to sing your name. Then the pyre with regal forms will burn all night long with a red flame, in order to declare my heart. The rivers will never bring henceforth as much sandalwod as I have given you for your house.

The Invisible Soul

It is while turning pale over books that I have found the secret.

Enclosed in the pentagram, the formulae pronounced, I had enveloped myself in shadow like a cloak; my soul was invisible from then on and passed through the pathways of the garden bordered by immortal acacias. It went furtively toward the visible souls that it loved, and kissed them on the mouth.

At other times it leaned over the banks of rivers and was amused by not seeing its reflection.

Over the grass dampened by the night, it glided like a breath toward the tombs ornamented with Egyptian inscriptions.

But the thieves of souls have come. Their clenched hands raise a black cape all the way to the eyes; their footfalls are felted, their hearts have the hatred of the disappeared.

They had espied my soul and knew the route that it was following; with murmured words they whispered to one another that it was there, without seeing it.

They have groped in the darkness, gestures reaching forward, eyes closed, and their brushing fingers have encountered my wings, and the wings have appeared.

The entire body of my soul had been gradually revealed. Fallen from mystery, it has touched the ground strewn with black flowers. Now it is a natural thing, and forever sad.

Posthumous Poem

I had already been dead for several hours, and I rose up toward the clouds, as souls do, thinking of the bizarre sadness in which I had left my friends. They had not been able to believe the verity of a black cup drunk, in order to forget certain ennuis that music, poets and walks under the necessary trees had been unable to cure.

For the moment, I rejoiced in the thought of seeing at close range the stars that I had once glimpsed from afar through black fireplaces, like little punch flames fluttering over the somber cup of the sky, and entirely occupied by my new impressions, I had almost forgotten the naughty child—oh, if only I could forget her!—when I saw a white form like me coming through the clouds, surely from the direction of the earth, which was rising slowly.

Ingenuously, she said: "It's me," and I read forever the dolorous book of her gaze; I saw that she was laughing, as a soul laughs, at my strange appearance, knowing full well that for herself, nothing could cause her to lose her heart-rending beauty.

"It's me," she said, "who was bored by your sad soul, and no longer having you to torment, O heart, O heart smitten forever, whom I never loved, but whom my infantile hands will cause to suffer for a long time yet in the other sphere, where a long time is called forever. And I've come."

Bewildered, I stammered: "You've come, you've come," no other word being able to render my trouble and my joy. Stars were doubtless passing by and fleeing toward infinity, without me even accompanying them with a regret. "You've come, and it's infinity, and it's your wicked eyes, and it's you. How gladly we're rising together toward the distant sky, toward the other sky, however distant it might be!"

But, O peevish paradise that doesn't appear! Does it even exist? In the meantime, it's raining, and your poor little soul is chilly in its white wings. How poorly white suits you! I'd rather have you with your dress as dark as your hair. But why? Is there a virginity in death? Bah! Virginity remains in someone whose heart will never vibrate. You're virgin of amour, my dear, virgin certainly for all of another eternity. We could recommence a new life, for never during the old one, when I knew you so cruelly, did you ever lose, even at the moment of the supreme spasm, the candor of unconsciousness that the divine flow of sensuality could not trouble in your eyes.

A Fantastic Tale[26]

In one of the most fabulous lands, there was an old king, with sumptuous and ridiculous garments, a young queen and an old court; things happened like that in all the lands of legend; ladies received the customary declarations under their rosy make-up and he people were overloaded by taxes. Apart from that, there were trees in the park, as many centuries old as one could desire.

The most important person in the court was the king's jester. His name was Mangetout, but no one knew why; he had a big ugly had with unkempt hair, and was conceited. That impertinent conceit increased strangely as soon as a lady was present. For reasons of taste, there were often ladies present. Mangetout spent his time composing puns and riddles, which he copied immediately in beautiful letters in a red notebook, with Indian ink for the riddles. When he was not working, he slept; when he was not sleeping, he smoked a pipe. He was an intellectual.

He was encountered in the kitchens sniffing the perfume of dishes and saucepans like an exegete of cookery. The master cooks with tall white pointed hats walked back and forth gravely. There were cats sitting on the knees of scullions in the embrasures of the windows and centenarian old women, all in black, crouching under the mantelpiece, their faces reddened by the fire.

---

[26] A revised version of this tale appeared in *La Vengeance du portrait ovale*, as "La Reine amoureuse" (tr. as "The Amorous Queen") but it is sufficiently different to justify translating the original version.

Mangetout, in his variegated garment and his pointed brodequins, arrived at the tables, cut large slices of bread and dipped them in the broth. He had grown very fat and he waddled. For the idiotic people his gluttony was an interesting and ever new subject of jokes.

One day, when melancholy leaves were falling in the wind from the great trees, due to the folly of autumn, the aforementioned young queen was allowing her blonde hair to stream over the golden balcony of her boudoir, leaning over toward the forest. At that moment, Mangetout passed by. It was like a scene from a drama; he was going to stuff his pipe with dry leaves. I have forgotten to mention that he was as miserly as he was ugly.

The queen was too pretty, but Mangetout did not see her, and as if great beauty demanded that a heart be captured by it, the queen's was, by the fault of the forest. Perhaps it is also necessary to blame her womanly nervous system. There were, in any case, all sorts of attenuating circumstances in the person of the jester, to explain why the queen had not perceived his beauty previously.

As soon as the queen had fallen in love, she went back into her boudoir and started to think sadly. Sitting in her sculpted chair on cushions of old golden velvet, she made a few very beautiful and very weary gestures, and then sent for her ladies in waiting and set forth to find the king. The halberdiers stood aside in the calm of the carpeted galleries, and beside the doors that she brushed, the pages in white satin garment began to weep plaintively.

"Madame," said the king, "it would displease our very courteous power to forbid you, being the queen, some sensuality or some dream, if it can be sumptuous. I only ask that the elect renders himself worthy of the great honor reserved for him. His instruction is very poor, his education deplorable; I will have him give the finest masters today. When he has become a great scholar, you can, without demeaning yourself, offer your imagination violins and the amorous fête that it desires."

The king's orders were executed immediately; the best masters were chosen, Mangetout learned fencing, Latin, Japanese, gymnastics and the piano. After that, to complete his education, he was sent to study rhetoric for a year at Louis-le-Grand. A curious thing happened; Mangetout, who hid a beautiful soul beneath his vulgar exterior, slowly acquired a taste for study; he became a grave man, in love with logic and the rigorous sciences. As the queen, unknown to the king, sent him a great deal of money, he had bought books and instruments of philosophy.

It seemed that his original ugliness had disappeared at the same time. Books had made him pale, he had allowed his hair to grow, and he no longer made puns. So, when he had to return, cries of admiration rose up throughout the realm. Carriages with large plumes emerged from the royal stables and turned majestically in order to go and fetch him, and along the avenue where grass outlined the paving stones, people in their best clothes waved their extended hands and their hoods, when the halberdiers opened the gala procession. Mangetout took the trouble to put on his court coat, and presented himself before the queen. During his absence, not seeing her, he had naturally fallen in love with her. He made her a very fine speech.

"He's no longer Mangetout," said the queen. "This one speaks to well; he has moreover, the air of a poet, with his long hair." And, turning toward him, sadly, she said: "I won't be able to love you."

One day, during Mangetout's absence, a new palfreyman had been engaged in the palace stables. He was very stupid but very robust. He it was who accompanied the queen when she went into the forest alone.

As soon as the king saw Mangetout and was informed of the queen's response, he was gripped by a great anger. "Madame," he said, "A queen ought to keep her promises; you have committed perjury, so you must die."

He immediately had the people summoned by the sound of trumpets to the terrace of the royal castle. A scaffold was set up draped in black velvet, around which torches in the hands of sad pages reddened the night, and the queen's head was cut off with a golden ax.

The executioner was very clumsy. No capital execution had ever taken place in the kingdom in human memory. The newspapers took advantage of it to attack the government violently. The function of executioner ceased, on that day, to be a sinecure. What a fine occasion to demand their suppression because of lack of necessity!

Mangetout regretted the queen greatly. His conduct on the day of the burial was beyond all eulogy. He had a fine lace handkerchief over his eyes constantly, and pronounced a few tactful words over the tomb. Then he handed in his resignation as jester, unable to live in a city that reminded him of such sad memories. He lived in a comfortable old house with old oak furniture and painted porcelains on the walls. In a large room whose windows overlooked the street, he smoked a long Dutch pipe. On the ceiling of the room there were large black sculpted beams, and pots of tulips of all colors on the window-sill, as in Rotterdam.

The Forest

I closed the gates of the City of Fear, where I had lived for many years. The crowd was densely packed between the tall black houses with red windows. On each roof there was an enormous candle with a violet flame; and the yellow wings of Chimeras were burned by the violet flames of the candles. They crackled delicately and fell to the ground as golden dust.

There were Chimeras everywhere, and Dreams were crouching behind the trees of the forest, looking at me with gleaming eyes. They were hideous little old men with broad fat faces and thin, twisted legs. They hopped about among the dead branches and sniggered in the night. I followed one of them who disappeared into a pathway. He was dressed in a long overcoat and a fur bonnet. A lantern with colored glass was swinging in his hand, with a smile between two ardent lips for a flame. He went forward, illuminating the realities with fantastic glimmers.

The little old man sometimes stopped in his march. He bent down at the foot of old trees and uprooted gigantic mushrooms. He took one, the dentellate edge of which he began to bite, in such a manner as to form the symmetrical indentations of an umbrella. Then he continued his walk, holding his lantern in one hand and the mushroom in the other, over which large raindrops fell with a monotonous sound.

Suddenly I saw the old man stop. His face went pale and his eyes were enlarged. He was writhing now, having thrown away the poisonous mushroom with an angry gesture. Then, after a few convulsions, he collapsed on the ground.

Then, from all the pathways of the forest, all the other paltry and fat-faced old men came running with long strides. They were carrying their lanterns in one hand and unbitten mushrooms in the other. And all of them, with lugubrious speeches and resigned but habitual eyes, set about covering the body of the poisoned Dream with dead leaves.

Prayer

You stand on the threshold of the temple and no one can approach you; it is you who assembles the clouds and creates the magical horizon, ever new.

O chimera, the first of the gods!

In order to render you sovereignly good, as offering are eternal and vain, we are now refusing you incense and the urns of other altars.

We will gladly sacrifice to you, O chimera, the things that are life. We will give you our youth and everything that suffers from loving.

Then the child Amour himself, with his light mouth of shadow and his suppliant limbs.

O chimera, first of the gods!

The Dark Star

Eyes have seen, I do not know in what country of nocturnal terrors, a dark star that resembles you. In what country, you say? In a land of marine algae, emerald and green torchlight.

In order to reach it, the road is one of those that can only be traveled in the evening, with a blindfold over the eyes and lips like the horizon.

The line of your lips resembles a beautiful red bird soaring. Before the adieux, distant voices will surely reach you, imploring in forgotten words.

Someone will come, bringing you roses, black roses for your mourning, pink roses for being, at the outset of a new voyage, the light burden of your hands.

Here are the ships of the great sea. The divine night presses your temples and plays in your heart. The oarsmen know that your youth is embarking for eternity...

For the land of marine algae, emerald and green torchlight.

The Urn

In the time when I was only formless clay in the hill, under the streams, the hand of the potter took me from my night of Erebus in order to enable me to contemplate the golden light of the sun. Now I am an urn with brown shiny sides, and olives, oil, Tyrian purple, perfumes and the divine ashes of the dead can be confided to me.

ALSO FROM BLACK COAT PRESS

( ) Marie Catherine d'Aulnoy. Tales of the Fays 1
( ) Marie Catherine d'Aulnoy. Tales of the Fays 2
( ) Honoré de Balzac. The Last Fay
( ) Mme Barbot de Villeneuve. The Naiads * Beauty and the Beast
( ) Cyprien Bérard. The Vampire Lord Ruthwen
( ) S. Henry Berthoud. The Angel Asrael
( ) Aloysius Bertrand. Gaspard de la Nuit
( ) Charlotte-Rose Caumont de La Force. The Land of Delights
( ) Comte de Caylus. The Impossible Enchantment
( ) Félicien Champsaur. Pharaoh's Wife
( ) Comtesse D.L. The Tyranny of the Fays Abolished
( ) Alexandre Dumas (w/Paul Lacroix). The Man who Married a Mermaid
( ) Marie-Antoinette Fagnan. The Enchanter's Mirror
( ) Paul Féval. Anne of the Isles
( ) Paul Féval: Knightshade
( ) Paul Féval: Revenants
( ) Paul Féval: Vampire City
( ) Paul Féval. The Vampire Countess
( ) Paul Féval. The Wandering Jew's Daughter
( ) Charles de Fieux, Chevalier de Mouhy. Lamekis
( ) Judith Gautier: Isoline and the Serpent-Flower
( ) Jules Janin. The Magnetized Corpse
( ) Gustave Kahn. The Tale of Gold and Silence
( ) Paul Lacroix. Danse Macabre
( ) Louis-Guillaume de La Follie. The Unpretentious Philosopher
( ) Etienne-Léon de Lamothe-Langon. The Virgin Vampire
( ) Etienne-Léon de Lamothe-Langon. The Mysterious Hermit of the Tomb
( ) Maurice Level. The Gates of Hell